# Mindtrapped!

He was young and impulsive.

He was hungry for fame and glory.

And he was stuck far from the center of things, in a tiny corner of the galaxy.

His kind could do wonders with their minds, so he had never known pain, fear, or loneliness. But now he had discovered them all — on a lush, primeval nothing of a world which would, in a hundred centuries or so, become known as "Earth." Now, he must suffer through eternity — or perhaps make a new beginning —

## in the body of a dog!

## Also by Neal Proud Deer

### fiction

*Trickle, Trickle, Fountain Flow*
*The Timechange Imperative*
*Survival of the Fittest*
*The Mingled Seed*
*Christmas Lost: A Fable*
(with Martin Pope)
*Hold Your Nose for America*
*& Other Stories*
*Cures, Crimes & Catastrophes*
(coming soon)
*Janus Warning* (in progress)

### non-fiction

*Lights...Camera...Arch!*
(with Foreword by John Goodman)
*Selling's Magic Words*
*The Black Press & the Search for Identity*
*Blacks and the Press*
*Race and the Times*
*Shalt Thou Kill?*
*The Centrality of Peace in Baha'ism*
*War and Thought*

# MINDTRAPPED!

## Neal Proud Deer

*To the Readers of Pawnee Public Library*

*— Read...read...read... and enjoy life!*

wordclay

*Neal*

Wordclay
1663 Liberty Drive, Suite 200
Bloomington, IN 47403
www.Wordclay.com

# MINDTRAPPED!

To Sport,
born when I was six,
he chased rabbits until he was 16
and died at 17,
after I had finished college

He was a marvelous companion
of my youth

## PROLOGUE

In the distance he could see Young Rover and Sport dauntlessly pursuing a cottontail. Gray turned slowly toward the cabin, then he paused and looked upward. In his mind's eye he could see the stars, now obscured by clouds, and the old longing returned. It had never really left him, but sometimes it lay dormant, and he could go days, weeks, months, even years without that dreaded loneliness.

"Gray. Oh, Gray... Over here." It was Susan calling him for supper.

"Gra-a-a-a-ay, where are you?"

Gray. Yes, he was "Gray." But he had known many names be-fore. There had been Remar, Nen, Chumack, Don, Gee, Miskah, and thousands of others. And there was Rover, of course. He had been Rover dozens of times. Man was often not very original when it came to naming his fellow animal companions.

"There you are, Gray. Come on, boy. Time to eat."

Susan was a good master, as they went. He had known better, but he had known many who were much worse. She talked softly to him, when she spoke, but most of the time she just kept silent. Tonight she seemed in a more talkative mood.

"You're getting to be a pretty old fellow, Gray. It's been almost fourteen years since I found you, and you were already grown then. You're going to have to learn you can't keep up with the younger dogs, anymore.

Most dogs your age just lie around. But not you. You'll never give up. You'll die on your feet, won't you, of boy?"

Yes, by man's reckoning, he was old — "ancient" after something more than 10,280 years. Treek was old. But, in dog terms, so was Susan's "Gray." He'd have to move out again soon, and he'd never see her again. Such departures were never easy, for, despite his efforts, Treek became emotionally attached to these humans. He knew he should be wary of man's treachery, but he had never learned to fully control his emotions.

How like the human legend of Cain he was, wandering the Earth to and fro, Treek felt. And, like Cain, he was paying for his sins. He had been paying for more than a hundred centuries. He realized now that the whole painful memory of his exile on Earth was about to repeat itself, but he could do nothing to stop its flooding from the dark recesses of his mind where he had managed to store it for many years.

Part I

# AMBITIONS TALL

pouch and pulled out a mind tape on quantitative physics. Maybe this would shift his concentration.

However, Dorn paused at the library table where he'd been sitting with Treek only long enough to pick up his pouch and leave.

Guilt. Guilt got him every time, Treek scolded himself. Dorn hadn't had even the slightest interest in what was in his head.

Treek slipped the physics transfer unit back into his pouch and slowly pulled his slender, nine-foot frame to a standing position. There wasn't much use going over this stuff anymore, he decided. How could he concentrate on physics or genetics or trilinear math when all that seemed important lay beyond?

He walked quickly from the mind library out onto the main campus. Excitement over his soon-to-be specialist status was swelling inside him. Never had he felt so close before. Never had he been so certain that his dreamed-of future would come to pass. He was at last convinced that he could escape Dejung's colorless world.

As he glided from the library, Treek took little note of the gleaming steel structures which formed the campus around him, nor of the glorious blue-green plantlife that dotted the area. He had seen it all hundreds of times before. Besides, these were a part of the life he would be leaving behind.

The warm, spring sun filtered through thin clouds and brought a sparkle to his ripple-textured, brown skin. An exuberant smile caressed his thin, smooth lips even as the three breathers located in his midsection inhaled Laazed's fresh, pure air. It seemed a perfect day, and it made Treek feel like running.

But his legs had not taken him far when his mood abruptly began to change. The air was still warm and fresh, and the sun was still shining brightly, but a gloom had begun to spread over his countenance. He had slowly, almost unconsciously, begun to open his mind fully as his happiness bubbled forth. Now something from outside his being was reaching in and destroying all the joy

he had known scant seconds earlier. Though he still felt confidence in his own ultimate success, some mind was reaching into his with thoughts of grief even before he could identify the sender or comprehend the message. Treek felt himself go rigid as the feeling pervaded. Immediately he wanted to close off his consciousness to this outside entity before it could deliver its message of sorrow. He wanted to flee to his own inner sanctuary of joy and hope. But he knew he could not escape the inevitable. Slowly, or what seemed slow to Treek, what felt like an eternity of fear and dread of the message's content — but which actually took place in the blinking of an eye — the sender and the message came clear to Treek. Instantly the sender's remorse was his own.

It was Dejung. His parent was reaching out to him with a message of almost unbearable sorrow: Zokken was dead! Gone forever! His mind was destroyed along with his body. There was no hope for renewal. His parent's only sibling was now but a thing of memory.

Dejung's thoughtwords formed slowly in Treek's mind. *"Of course, there is no replacing him."* Then, there was a pause in his parent's thought-projection which began to stretch on into forever, a pause which actually lasted less than a second. *"There could never be another like Zokken. But he's alive in our memory. He'll remain there through all time. There can be no destroying that."*

Treek knew this was true. It was obvious. Why waste time on intellectual drivel?

*"But how? What happened?"* he demanded.

Immediately his mind was flooded with the details of the devastating planetary accident on Troaj which took not only Zokken but hundreds of other natives of Laazed as well.

Treek could feel Dejung's remorse flooding his mind. There was another strong emotion there too, but Treek would not let it past the doorway into his mind.

And there was something else. Something which he was slowly becoming aware of — and resenting. There were other minds — observers — sitting in the periphery of his intellect. Treek realized that they must have been there all along, but the strength of Dejung's emotion had all but masked them from perception. Now, Treek felt the presence of the others of his parent's marriage group — Carris, Taw, and Lozar. He had never really understood their relationship to his parent — or disliked it more. Sure, he could accept it intellectually. Unlike the so-called "single-sexers" his people had encountered elsewhere in the galaxy, he knew that all Laazenes, as duo-sexuals, served as total parents. They did not require the union of the body, as those others did, to give birth to their young. Each Laazene fertilized his own eggs so there was one parent for each child. All this seemed only natural. What he had never been able to comprehend emotionally was the need for this "marriage of the minds." He knew from his study of Laazene history that because they were duo-sexuals, his people had begun their existence at the dawn of time as thoroughly independent entities. There had never been any need for a closeness of the body, as the male and female "single-sexers" required; perhaps, some theoreticians had rationalized, this was why Laazenes were so ripe for the development of telepathic thought. For, with it, there was never any need for any among his kind to be alone again. But why this total commitment — this "marriage"? Why was it necessary for some to establish permanent "mind links" with others, removing all thought-blocks completely? Dejung had three such partners to whom he never closed his thoughts. And all four of them huddled together in Treek's mind for what might have been a very long time, but wasn't. Finally, one by one, they began to slip out of his head. Last of all, Dejung departed, leaving him alone with his melancholy and memories.

Eventually his thoughts slipped back to happier days. Perhaps as no other, Zokken had influenced his young life. At 67, Treek was now, at best, only slightly over halfway — maybe two-thirds — through his program at the Deame Institute for Galactic Studies, and he had Zokken to thank for his being here to begin with. Zokken had given a purpose to life and also a direction for him to follow. It had been Zokken who had filled him with excitement about the stars. It had been Zokken who had encouraged his interest in galactic studies. And it had been Zokken who had even helped him prepare for study at Deame. Now, Zokken was gone — *betrayed* by those beloved stars he had served so well.

*"There is no joy like a star explorer's joy,"* Zokken had told him on his last visit to Laazed 11 years before. Treek had not actually seen him then, but his mentor's mind had sought him out from across the globe and spoken to him. Treek realized now that it had been almost 19 years since he had last seen Zokken.

*"It's the joy of discovery out there,"* Zokken had said. *"You're experiencing something new. Sometimes you come in contact with life forms and worlds our people couldn't even conceive. There is nothing to compare with it on Laazed. Here, everything has been done before; every thought has been thought before. But, out there, you have a chance for something really new, really exciting. Not like those canned simulation experiences you have here. Everything out there is REAL!"* Zokken laughed hardily with his mind and added: *"Why, I may never give up my stellar explorations. I may decide to live*

*forever. How many other Laazenes have you ever heard
say that?"*

Treek had to admit it was a novel concept — living
forever. He'd never known anyone who wanted to live
forever. Most chose oblivion after two or three thousand
years — or the long sleep. And few of those who came
out after five or ten thousand years of slumber lasted
long. They were soon bored with their existence again
and chose oblivion or more sleep. But here was one so
excited with life after almost two thousand years of it
that he talked of living forever.

It wasn't fair. One who wanted to live so badly and
was so excited about life should not be called away to
oblivion without first choosing it.

His thoughts continued, drifting and wafting through
his memories of Zokken.

A few hours later, Treek found himself — along with
2,000 others — in the clouds, zooming over Laazed.
They had already completed well over half the 31,000-
mile trip and would be landing in a matter of moments.
Treek had chosen a window seat and stared as the
planetary craft slipped downward over the glowing,
metallic towers of Hulmar, Laazed's largest city, home of
38 million minds, one-seventh of whom were in
prolonged slumber after a lifetime of activity. The sun
was shining warmly as it had earlier in the day on the
opposite side of the planet, but its brightness could no
longer reach into Treek's consciousness.

He felt really alone now. More alone than he had ever
before felt in his 67 years. Yet he kept his mind closed
to outside thought. Since those first few moments when
Dejung had contacted him and then broke away, Treek
had kept all others' thoughts out of his mind. He
wanted to share his memories of Zokken with no one.
They were his alone. Even Dejung could not share that
special relationship which he and Zokken had made for

themselves. Especially not Dejung. So he was alone now — by choice. The feeling was oppressive and haunting, yet it was his, and somehow he felt a glory in it as his mind flashed back, back, back into the past.

The planetary craft continued gliding down toward Hulmar until the city's metal architecture surrounded them. There was a harmony in this, a city so large yet unified in theme and form. Treek had felt it as he grew from childhood here, but somehow now its beauty and simplicity were lost to him. In the distance, Treek could barely make out the complex of buildings where Dejung, the cultural historian, lived and worked day-after-day, year-after-year, century-after-century. Always the same. Treek knew his parent must be yearning for him now, hungry for his mind. The blank wall of consciousness which he must feel surely was frustrating and grieving him even more. Treek felt a sudden touch of guilt. He had not purposely meant to hurt Dejung. He had only wanted — needed — to be alone with his thoughts and memories. Perhaps he had been wrong to shut Dejung out of his mind.

Suddenly he thrust the flood gates open. He broke the lock and a conglomeration of emotions came pouring into his mind.

*"I've been waiting for you,"* someone thoughtsaid immediately. It was his parent, as he knew it would be, *"I knew you'd come. But why did you close me out?"*

*"I'm sorry. I just had to be alone — to remember him...as I knew him,"* Treek replied. It was hard for him to form the thoughts clearly. But it didn't matter, anyway. Dejung couldn't understand.

*"Yes, he was special — to you. AND to me! You never knew how close we were as children. And as we grew older. He was the senior, and I depended on him. I never wanted him to go. I told him I needed his strength, but he laughed and left for the stars. He left me alone. I never*

*forgave him for that."* Dejung paused briefly, then continued solemnly. *"I should have. I know that now. That was almost 20 centuries ago. Now...it's too late!"*

Dejung's thoughts broke off and were replaced by raw emotion. Suddenly Treek saw that his parent's hurt equaled his own. Now it was time for him to offer comfort and compassion, but he could not.

The craft landed momentarily, and Dejung was there to meet Treek in person, a fact that further punctuated their mutual loss. The younger Laazene slipped quickly off the craft, and Dejung ran to embrace him. Then the parent spoke aloud. The sound of of the other's voice seemed strange and unreal to Treek who could not remember the last time he had heard it. Mental contact between them had decades ago almost completely replaced the spoken word. But now the formality of the spoken language seemed strangely appropriate.

After a few simple words of greeting, Dejung added: "I hope this will not be too great an interruption of your studies."

Treek knew that there was much more to the statement than the words implied, but since Dejung had chosen the verbal form, Treek did not try to delve into his parent's mind.

"It can be made up. However long I take off can be made up."

Other travelers scurried about them. As he and Dejung turned to walk from the main lobby of the travel port, Treek opened his reception to capacity and felt the full force of the myriad of minds with their many and diverse thoughts. One very near Treek had had a particularly disturbing mental clash with a close friend. Another worried about his work. Still another was steeped in the manic-depressive emotions of jealousy and resentment.

Thank goodness his ancestors had learned ways to

shelter themselves from this mental anarchy, Treek told himself, rushing to slam his mind's door on all the mental clatter. The conglomeration of thought clutter — if it went unchecked — could drive one crazy in a matter of hours, and it had been known to do so. Treek marveled again, as he had done so often before in his short lifetime, at all the wondrous accomplishments of his race — not least of which was the varied use of the mind. How often he had taken for granted the ability to reach into another's mind and pull out not only his thoughts but his emotions as well. And a Laazene's telekinetic abilities were unparalleled in diversity, though there were many ethical and practical restrictions placed on their usage. The mind was indeed a marvelous instrument, and he had come to appreciate it even more during his years of study at Deame. There were countless trillions of creatures in the known cosmos, yet his people had never found another so adept in mental abilities. Why there seemed practically nothing which a Laazene couldn't do with his mind if he but tried. A sudden renewal of race pride rushed over Treek, but it was brought low as he felt other minds enter his — those of Carris and Taw — and again he was reminded why he had returned here.

As he and Dejung climbed into the overland shuttle, Treek thought again of Zokken and the universe of stars he had called home. How he longed to be out there himself at this very moment.

Instantly, he felt a surge of shock from another of the minds which monitored his thoughts.

*"How can you still feel that way after what happened to Zokken?"* It was Taw. *"Surely you don't plan to continue your study there! You must know — "* There was an abrupt breakoff of the transmission, as though the sender were biting a mental tongue to keep his thoughts from bursting forth. Treek knew Taw had always

opposed his plans, but now he felt as though the other must be speaking more out of sympathy for Dejung.

A great mental silence followed. No one was placing thoughts into Treek's mind. He felt empty, alone, depressed, but somehow elated all at once. How could he ever tell Taw how he felt? Even though the other could reach into the depths of his mind, he could not actually experience Treek's longings for himself. Now there was also Zokken's death and the reality of a tragedy which had a direct bearing on all his plans and hopes for the future. It seemed as though his desire for a career among the stars had been a part of his life forever, but should he be having second thoughts in light of what had happened? If Zokken had not gone out there, he would be alive today. But would he have been the same Zokken Treek had known and grown to love as a child if he had never been a stellar explorer?

Treek could feel a knocking at the door to his mind, and he realized that he had unconsciously almost completely closed out all traffic in thoughts, leaving room only for others to peep in, but not enter with their own thoughts. Gradually, now, he slid that door open, and he found his parent outside, waiting.

"*No, Treek, I was wrong once before,*" Dejung thoughtsaid. And Treek realized his parent must have been monitoring the thoughts that he had not been allowed to interrupt. "*You're right. The Zokken you loved would not have been the same if he had been shackled to Laazed, and I was wrong in trying to hold him here. He lived enough out there for ten lifetimes. No, Treek, you must go too. There is a great destiny waiting for you somewhere out there among those distant solar systems. You must go and find it!*"

But Treek knew Dejung really wished he would stay.

## CHAPTER TWO

"There is no question about your ability, Treek. Your work in the preliminary program was outstanding, and during the two years you have been engaged in advanced studies, you have performed much more than adequately. But we just do not feel that you should be granted advanced placement. There are still too many gaps in your knowledge that must be filled before you can be placed in the concluding phase of your educational program. I'm sorry. Your request must be denied."

Treek had already guessed the nature of the panel's decision. Such oral statements were usually reserved for formal pronouncements. Had the council decided otherwise, no doubt some of their minds would have been open to him, and he would have been able to read their decision long before the chairman spoke it.

"Is there no appeal?" he asked, responding in the same emotionless, matter-of-fact manner.

"Yes, you may take this to the Institute General Board, if you like, but I hardly think they will disagree with our findings. Please understand: This should not be considered as a negative reflection on your performance. You are a fine student. We are pleased with the work you have done at Deame. I am convinced that you will make an outstanding contribution in stellar research someday. Further, it is the judgment of this panel that you will be ready to begin internship in 10 years, and we are entering this statement in your general record.

"Remember, Treek, you are still a very young person. We have people at the Institute five times your age, you know."

The chairman halted his pronouncement. His bumpy, gray skin glistened, and his middle breather rose and fell rapidly, indicating he was breathing deeply. Treek could not tell if this was a deliberate act or if his breathing was part of some ritual. Finally, the other resumed his statement.

"Treek, our people in the stellar program — all phases — must be thoroughly prepared. They must be our finest citizens. After all, they are our ambassadors to the universe. They will be contacting and negotiating with all forms of life out there" — the chairman raised his sturdy left hand and made a general sweep toward the sky as he glanced upward — "and they must be able to represent our race with pose and the best and most complete education we can give them."

He smiled again and looked directly into Treek's olive-toned eyes. Treek sensed this was the end of his statement, so he rose from the chair in which he had been sitting, thanked the chairman and the other members of the panel, then excused himself.

The chairman had gone to great length to point out that the council's decision was not intended as a rebuke of his ability, and Treek knew this should be a sign of encouragement, but he couldn't bring himself to feel encouraged just at this moment. In the three years since Zokken had died, he had applied himself diligently. He took little time off for entertainment. He had worked and waited for this moment. Throughout it all, he had known that advanced placement into the concluding phase was a difficult thing to achieve;

however, he had been convinced he could make it. During the past year, he had felt more and more sure of himself. Now, the council had made a formal pronouncement of internship — he would have to wait ten more years.

Treek walked slowly as he left the Monlar Hall of Hope, built millennia  ago as Deame's first structure and designed to symbolize the optimism his people felt about the future of space research. Its ornate curves contrasted sharply with the simple, modern lines of most of the other campus buildings. Still, with its central tower — like a giant hand raised upward almost a mile toward the heavens — it was one of the world's leading architectural wonders. Currently the structure housed only Deame's administrative offices, and certainly Treek did not feel the hope that the structure was supposed to convey.

The temperature outside was pleasant, even as it had been on the day he had heard of Zokken's death. On that occasion, his mind had been saturated with excitement when he'd felt the touch of another mind bringing sadness. Today, Treek felt the gloom of defeat and disappointment. But he again felt the twinge of another's thoughts inside his head.

He gradually increased his gait as he moved toward the inner circle of dormitories and his own chambers. As he walked, the feeling that he was being watched — even spied upon — added an odd and eerie quality to his movements. There was no identifying the observer inside his mind, but Treek knew he was there watching but refusing to move close enough to reveal his identity. Treek realized he could slam this phantom out of his mind and resume his solitude, but, strangely, he had no desire to do that. His initial feeling of fear was replaced by anger, and he suddenly lashed out at the mental intruder.

*"Who are you? Why are you watching me?"*
There was no response.
*"What have I done to cause you to spy on me?"*
Still no answer. The other mind's presence remained detectable at the corners of his thoughts, however. The integrity of the individual mind had always been paramount in Laazene telepathy. Now Treek felt strangely put upon and violated. His fury welled.
*"What is it? Are you afraid to identity yourself? Are you a mental weakling too poor to live by your own thoughts — so poor you have to steal others'?"*
Desperately he tried every trick he could think of to get the other to draw himself out. Finally his efforts were rewarded.
*"At least I don't delude myself with shallow dreams of glory!"* the intruder murmured inside his mind. Immediately Treek realized this was a stranger. The thought pattern was entirely unfamiliar.
Then gradually, as the meaning of this outsider's statement dawned on Treek, a new hostility ignited within his being. A feeling near hatred gripped him, a gnawing and disturbing dislike for one whom he had never even met, either physically or mentally.
*"What are you accusing me of?"* he demanded.
There was no direct response to his question, but Treek had the distinct impression that the other was laughing at him.
A third party — also a stranger to Treek — abruptly interposed himself into the conflict of wills. *"I'm sorry, Treek, but Guin didn't have the right to do this."*
There was a momentary pause while this other broke away from his mind. Treek supposed he was speaking privately to the first intruder. Then the third party returned to him.
*"I'm Pera, a galactic anthropology student, also at Deame. I'll try to prevent this from happening again. I*

*must share part of the responsibility for this intrusion into your private space. Both of us will withdraw now."*

Treek could feel the other minds begin to slip away. Suddenly he reached out and tugged at them.

*"No! Stop!"* he thoughtshouted. *"You can't leave before you tell me why — why you were doing this!"*

*"No harm was intended, I assure you,"* Pera replied. *"It began as part of a simple thought-sweep for my studies. I came across you quite by accident. I found out about your family and your difficulties with them and what happened to Zokken. I told Guin about you, and he began to monitor your thoughts regularly. I asked him to stop, but he insisted that you pertained to his studies — he's working in omni-psychology — that you are a cultural throwback because of your impatient nature and your ardent zeal for life — and because you are apparently such a loner. Perhaps what he did — what WE did — was wrong. I promise it will not happen again."*

Somewhere in the midst of Pera's thought transmission, Treek felt Guin's mind break away. Then Pera's was gone also. The whole experience left him bewildered and his anger still smoldering.

Just as abruptly as he had broken off, Pera returned.

*"Treek, we — or rather I — would like to do more than just apologize to you. I'd like very much to meet you physically. I'd like for Guin — for both of us — to meet you, face-to-face. If you refuse, I'll understand why."*

But Treek found himself agreeing to the meeting. He was still very angry about the intrusion into his own personal thought space, but he wanted to find out more about the research these two were conducting — to meet this Guin and find out what he had meant by those ridiculous accusations. Certainly Treek realized he was possessed by a heartfelt longing to touch the stars, a desire he had known since childhood when he'd first heard Zokken tell of his wondrous adventures. He realized also that that longing had not lessened since Zokken's death. If anything, it had intensified. He couldn't explain why. He didn't himself understand why. It was just there, beckoning him to what must be a great future. Now, there were these two intruders to deal with. He wanted this meeting because, in a face-to-face challenge, they could not escape his wrath. Perhaps there was another reason why he would keep this appointment, but he would not let himself believe it.

# CHAPTER THREE

*"Have either of you ever seen a pontimar?"* Guin asked, then continued before the others could respond. *"No matter. The thing's about four feet long, has a pointed, ugly snout, and is completely hairless."*

An obviously distorted image of the creature flashed immediately through Treek's mind. He was about to indicate his amusement when Guin continued the account inside his head.

*"But that's not the worst. You can't see the worst thing about the creature. I found out about it the hard way. On my visit with Skakor fourteen years ago, I really found out about it! I thought getting away into the wilds of Marzam would be a wonderful break. I thought, 'What could be more refreshing than visiting my friend on that animal preserve?' Well, I found out. And it was the pontimar that pointed the way.*

*"What's the worst thing about the pontimar, you ask. Well, it's completely slick. Its whole body is covered with some kind of oil or grease or something. We chased that creature for what must have been three hours — over hills, through streams, around trees. Everywhere! And then when one of us would grab it, it'd*
just slip away from us and be gone again. Skakor finally went back and got its mate — the beast's a monosexual, you see — and with the other pontimar on a leash, we finally lured the first one back to its own area.

an intellectual glimmer of what it meant to mingle the minds "as one."

However, the stories of Zokken never strayed far from his memory.

And the things he was learning in his class work further fired his zeal to be on to his "life's work." He studied about the major star routes, about the dangers of black holes, of the many poisonous creatures of Zedkim VI and the murderous treachery of the semi-savage inhabitants of the three planets of the Lyllium system. He learned the fundamentals of the simple Outer Skin for use in poisonous environments, and of the more cumbersome Aura when more protection was needed.

Through all his training, though, his instructors emphasized the further development of the mind and its many uses. He found that much of what was prohibited on Laazed did not apply in exploratory work, and he practiced exercises to develop brain power. He learned about mental tasks his ancestors would hardly have dreamed of. Like mind control over lower beings (which far surpassed the simple telesuggestion techniques he'd learned as a child). And teletransference, or the ability to actually transfer his intellect into the body of another organism. The teletransference technique was usually utilized only when irreparable damage had been done the body. Through it, the electrical impulses that form the mind were transferred into the body of another Laazene where they could be temporarily housed. Such transference could even be accomplished using lower organisms; however, there was a danger that the two alien minds might become inseparably intertwined if not separated in a short time.

All this seemed wild and exciting and made Treek wish Zokken were alive to share his knowledge and recount actual stories of the amazing powers of the mind.

As he studied, Treek came to no longer marvel at Guin and Pera's "illegal" entry into his own mind, for he felt tempted himself to try out his newly developing powers. But he stopped short when he remembered the warning of his instructor, Namar:

*"The mind is a sacred thing. It is not a toy. It is not a weapon. It is a tool, the greatest tool known to our race. We must never abuse this tool because its powers have been developed and delivered to us by our ancestors as a sacred trust!"*

His teacher was, of course, right, though Treek could hardly wait to have cause to use these abilities, nevertheless.

*"Most of these powers of mind will never be used by most*

*of you,"* Namar thoughtsaid, addressing his Mental Control class, of which Treek was a participant. *"But the real wonder is that they will be available to you should you ever need to use them. To be ready, in case you do need them, you must study diligently and master the powers against that day when they may save your life."*

But instead of making Treek want to study harder, the knowledge he had already acquired made him increasingly anxious to achieve his goals. Again he began to seek a shortcut, a search which was fruitless and frustrating for many months.

Eventually, however, it found him.

## CHAPTER FOUR

The oppressively heavy air of Colmar seemed to block Treek's breathers and clog his lungs. He found himself gasping desperately just to pull in sufficient air to stay alive. He hardly felt alert. Near him sat Pera, shivering in the planet's cold, damp air. Several feet away, in a makeshift shelter they had hastily thrown together out of torn clothing salvaged from their ship, Guin alternately slept and shouted his delirium.

*"He isn't getting any better. Two days like this. If anything, he's worse,"* Treek thoughtsaid.

Pera nodded in agreement, but offered no comment. His shivering seemed to grow gradually more pronounced.

They sat in silence for a long while. It seemed totally strange — unreal — for Guin not to be entertaining them with one of his outlandish accounts. Pera did not seem quite himself either. But Treek realized he'd never known these two in a situation quite like this before. Something in his mind urged him to reach out to Pera with words of comfort and affection; however, he did not.

*"We'll have to do something soon. Our nourishment won't hold out much longer if we just sit around hoping for rescue,"* he added, finally.

Still Pera said nothing.

*"I've been checking the remains of our surface maps.*

*Thaark's Dija settlement can't be more than a hundred miles over that way."* He pointed generally westward. *"On the other side of those mountains. Maybe twenty miles beyond."*

Pera seemed to be staring off into nothingness, so Treek dropped his pitch. He'd come back to it later, but not much later. He knew they'd have to do something soon.

He thought back on the series of events that had brought the three of them to Colmar in the first place. It had been his idea. An outing. A short vacation. A chance to be together physically as well as mentally and to be away from the constant scholastic pressures of Deame. They had taken a light cruiser and set out on the less-than-one-day journey to Zil, but something had happened to the ship's controls — they weren't sure what — as they entered the outer fringes of the Barrik system. Zil was the second planet from the sun, but it became increasingly apparent they could never make it that far. So they plunged into the atmosphere of Colmar, the fourth planet, hoping to land and make repairs, then be on their way again. But the ship had shattered on impact. They had been lucky to escape with their lives.

They'd slipped into Outer Skins, but these had been damaged in the crash and served only to offer some protection from the cold, too badly torn to act as breather suits. Guin had suffered multiple bruises and cuts, so Treek and Pera built a temporary shelter. That had been five days ago. Strangely, Guin had slipped into unconsciousness two days ago and had become delirious. But even more strange was their inability to make mental contact with the settlers at Dijan. Perhaps it had something to do with the Thaarkian mental wavelength — Treek had never met a native of Thaark, so he wasn't sure — or something to do with the atmosphere of Colmar, but both possibilities seemed remote.

Treek decided to try again with Pera.

*"I could go alone over the mountains and attempt to bring back help. It would be much faster that way, but it might be..."* He paused, recomposing his thoughts before continuing. *"...might not be best for you two."* Another pause. *"No, I think we'll all have to go together."*

Pera looked up and spoke at last. *"But how?"*

Treek knew his companion was thinking of the third member of their party.

*"We'll have to carry him. Surely we can rig something. We can share the load, or take turns. Whatever. But we can't wait much longer. We should go now, as soon as we can get everything ready. Maybe, with luck, in another five days we'll be in Dijan."*

He was gearing up for a lengthy debate, but Pera replied simply: *"I agree."*

Two hours later, they were starting out on their journey, with Guin strapped into a kind of harness slung between them. By then, it was already afternoon, and Treek knew they would have little time to travel before the sun set, when it would become impossible to move across the rugged terrain. Besides, after dark, the temperature fell drastically on this world. They would not want to be moving about in their battered suits then. For these and other reasons, Treek was determined to make as much progress as possible before nightfall. He was in the lead, and he set a brisk pace, the terrain being more or less level and smooth at this point in their journey, with some scattered brush but little other vegetation. He anticipated their beginning the assault of the mountains some time the following day.

They moved on methodically, with little communication between them, for some time. Occasionally Guin would rant about something, but his companions hardly broke pace. By late afternoon, Treek estimated they had traveled about five miles. He could see that the litter arrangement was slowing them considerably.

"Oh, my head!" Guin mumbled, speaking aloud, but he seemed at last to be conscious. "Where am I?" Then he broke into thought projection: *"Pera, Treek, what's happening?"*

Treek glanced around at Guin and came to a halt.

*"It's all right, Guin. We're taking you to Thaark colony Dija. How do you feel?"* Treek replied, refusing to plunge completely into his friend's psyche.

*"Weak. I'm weak. And this pain in my head is devastating. How long have I been out?"*

*"Two-and-a-half days,"* Pera answered. *"You'd better rest and save your strength for telekinetic healing. You've got to bring your mental focus around to that. Evidently you've been in so deep, you've made little progress in coming around."*

*"I know, and I can't understand it. My body should have mended itself by now, with or without my concentration. Something's wrong: I'm not getting any better. I feel worse than before."*

*"You rest now. You'll feel the healing soon,"* Treek responded, then privately to Pera, he added: *"I think it has something to do with this planet. Maybe it's the air or the soil or the vegetation. I don't know, but I've felt it too. I haven't been getting over the minor injuries I received either."*

*"I know, I — "*

"Ay-e-e-e! My head! Not now, Pera! Look! There's a shabbon and a pontimar. What? No-o-o-o! Not now!"

*"He's slipped away from us again,"* Treek thoughtsaid.

*"Yes."*

They decided to set up their temporary shelter where

they had halted because Colmar's red sun had already slipped behind the mountain range, and the night cold had begun to take over. After they had erected the shelter, Treek and Pera ate silently. Then Pera tried to pour some cold soup down Guin's throat, but most of it spilled onto the dry Colmaric soil.

The wasted soup might cost them, Treek reminded himself. They couldn't afford such waste. He started to drop the thought into Pera's head, but he held back. His companion was doing the best he could. He felt suddenly guilty he had even thought that.

Soon, the two joined the third in slumber, but Treek awoke several times during the bitter Colmaric night, his muscles aching, and the frigid temperatures biting at his extremities. Somehow this didn't seem right either. His mind should be able to make his body more comfortable. However, no amount of thinking about what should be seemed to set the situation right, so he would doze off, only to shiver himself awake again soon.

By the middle of the following day, the three of them had begun the ascent of the mountains. Guin had not again regained consciousness, and his body did not seem yet to be healing, as it should have. In fact, he seemed even more frail and delirious. With each step he and Pera took up the mountainside, it became increasingly apparent to Treek that they would have to find another method for transporting their ailing companion. They were about halfway up one of the major foothills when Treek brought the party to a halt on a ledge, pointing out this problem to Pera.

*"We could take turns carrying him,"* the other suggested.

*"I'm afraid we'll have to, but it'll be difficult on these steep grades for the one supporting Guin. Maybe we can think of another way later."*

They had just finished unstrapping Guin. Treek was

sitting on a smooth rock preparing to tie his friend in a new harness on his back when the other's black eyes sprang open.

"Now! Now!" Guin shouted as he leaped to his feet.

*"Delirious again!"* Pera projected to Treek. *"Grab him!"* But as Treek reached to pull his friend back downward, Guin jerked, stumbling backwards on wobbly legs. By the time both Treek and Pera were also standing, he was several feet away, staggering shakily.

"No! Don't come near me," Guin shouted frantically, his eyes showing fear and confusion, as well as delirium.

*"Stop! Please, Guin, wait! We're your friends,"* Pera pleaded.

But their companion's gaze flashed wildly from one of them to the other, and he continued to creep backwards.

Treek caught the glimmer of horror in Pera's eyes, as he made a frantic lunge toward their delirious companion. But he arrived too late.

Guin stumbled backwards again and went plummeting, rotating rapidly, toward a jagged and rocky ravine below. His fall seemed to last an eternity as his two friends peered over the cliff after him, but Guin uttered not a single sound as he fell.

Nor did Treek or Pera speak for several moments thereafter. They just stood, frozen by grief, peering over at the shattered body of their friend. Treek's probing mind told him there was no life remaining in the crumpled figure, but he did not want to accept what he knew was a certainty. Finally, he glanced briefly at Pera and thoughtspoke.

*"His mind..."* he began, but he realized Pera was still searching desperately.

*"No,"* Pera replied at last. *"He was too delirious. He didn't know what was happening. He may not even have*

possibly be transferred from surveying into exploration even before his internship was scheduled to begin under his old program. Also, if he distinguished himself in survey work, he might be able to write his own ticket to a better position, not just accept whatever they threw at him.

"...Most of you have shown yourselves as outstanding students here at Deame. Otherwise, you would not have been considered for this accelerated program. So we expect good work from you. Once again, welcome to the gateway to the stars."

The commander had completed his remarks. But Treek wondered how much of that was true — about being outstanding students. How many who applied for survey work were turned away? If they were as desperate as they seemed... But he knew he had performed well, so perhaps there was something to what Landor had said. Now it was up to him to prove himself again, however, because he knew there was no resting on his past performance.

During the days and weeks that followed, he found himself buried in work, requiring him to perform at a pace far beyond any which he had previously known. He quickly realized that "accelerated" meant learning in a few months what normally might take years to grasp. Certainly there were shortcuts, but only the minor aspects of the program were skimmed over. All the major materials were covered in detail.

He had known that survey engineers preceded the major exploratory teams, that their findings helped the others decide where to go and with how many and with what equipment. But he had not realized there was so much to know about surveying star systems and planets. He learned that there were sometimes several stages of survey work even before the exploratory teams made up their minds about whether or not to journey to a given planet. And some star systems had much greater survey priority than others because of their locations on or near the primary space channels.

Now he had to learn much more about mathematics, chemistry, physics, atmospheric standards, and mineral uses. Because survey teams spent much less time in actual contact with alien races, his program of study touched much less heavily on cultural anthropology and mental development than did the explorer's program. Treek missed these subjects, but he felt certain he would have ample opportunities to learn more in these areas once he transferred out of surveying and became an active explorer.

After about three months of accelerated planetary survey studies at Deame, Treek and the other new recruits were taken on their first field trip. The actual journey took less than a day. Treek had gone further than Capra VII on several occasions, but he was, nevertheless, very excited about the visit. It was his first real trip as an explorer. Oh, he knew he wasn't really an explorer. He wasn't even a surveyor yet. But, for the first time, he knew it was real. He had heard all those stories of Zokken. He had read about stellar research for decades. And he had been a Deame student for almost 24 years. But nothing had ever felt this real before.

Treek knew that Capra VII was overrun with Deame students. Hundreds came here every year to engage in all manner of simple training programs. He also knew that if he had remained in the explorer program, he would have visited this very planet on one of his first field trips in elementary exploration. There were no higher life forms on Capra VII, so explorer students didn't go beyond the basics on the planet, but since there existed all manner of minerals, plantlife, and lower animal forms not found on Laazed, it made an excellent place for survey students to study.

Or so he was told.

During this first trip out, Treek and his classmates did not actually do any survey work. They spent most of their three days there getting used to alien soil and listening to their teachers instruct them on the fine points of surveying.

Later, on subsequent field trips to Capra VII, they had plenty of opportunities to demonstrate their newly acquired knowledge. Still later, they moved on to other planets in the Capra system as well as planets in the Mozak and Dufeld systems.

On Dufeld II, also known as Orenz, they found a world of clean, sparkling oceans and very high mountain peaks. The valleys were inhabited by quadrupeds of high intelligence in the early stages of cultural development. However, because of its variant soil, there was no animal life in the upper elevations. Dressed in their Outer Skins, they were performing tests of the climatic conditions and chemical makeup of the soil on one of the planet's highest plateaus. Nearby, their instructor, Tak, watched, and, from time to time, threw a thought their way.

*"Certainly Orenz is not unique. You'll undoubtedly encounter many worlds with widely contrasting conditions,"* he thoughtsaid. *"However, there are few with this type of purple, acidic soil. It makes Orenz's mountain peaks at once both barren but beautiful to look upon from a distance and, at the same time, deadly up close to those who don't treat them with the proper respect."*

Treek noted Tak's statement, but he made little effort to concentrate on it. He had heard it all before. Instead, his mind was overwhelmed with excitement as he thought of landing on some distant world previously unseen by an Laazene. There would be a frenzy of activity as he and his colleagues set about preparing themselves for the great discoveries. And when they had found these, what glory there would be! Their fame would spread far across the galaxy.

He rushed from one test to the next, but his mind was far away. He was hardly aware of it when his foot slipped on a loose stone on the steep mountainside.

Abruptly, he was sliding down the rocky mountain. His mind quickly came to focus on his situation but only as he plunged over the edge of a steep cliff.

*Down!*

Down he plunged. His feet first, then his head. Swiftly he rotated over and over as he dropped. Below him — far away, but closing rapidly — was a huge pile of jagged rocks. Just as had "killed" Guin in that simulat. Only this wasn't a simulation.

*This was reality!*

Desperately he reached out to break his fall, but he couldn't catch himself as he plummeted. He was much too far from the mountainside.

He could touch nothing but air! Instantly he knew the inevitable. He was falling to his death!

Barely seconds of his life remained unless he could do something. His thin Outer Skin would hardly save him when he crashed into those hot, acidic rocks.

His mind! Yes, he must be able to save himself.

His thoughts flowed outward immediately. Had his descent into oblivion slowed? No, he was still falling at full speed. The pile of rocks seemed very near, and he could do nothing!

Now he saw a vision of faces before him — Guin and Pera, a ghostly Zokken, and even Dejung. They were all imploring him to keep trying.

He redoubled his efforts. Desperately, now — almost angrily — he reached into his memory attempting to pull out what he knew of telekinesis that would save him. But he couldn't bring it forth. He did not know

## CHAPTER SEVEN

All his special training was behind him. The formal graduation program would take place in less than a week, and already some of his classmates had received their duty assignments. At least one, Davimar, had been asked to skip the graduation exercises and had already left to assume his post. Others were scheduled to leave immediately after graduation.

Treek sat quietly in his room early one morning, the ridges of his rippled, brown skin sharply defined as they always were when he became tense or excited. He had attempted to process some mental notes, but he could not clearly focus his attention on the school work. Only three days remained before graduation now, and rumor had spread that the remaining duty assignments would be made today. He hoped so. The suspense of the wait seemed to prolong each moment into an hour and each hour into a week. Fully three-fourths of his classmates had received their assignments, and he could not understand why his had not yet been announced. His work in the program had been very good, but he knew that assignments were not made solely on the basis of grades. Perhaps his was to be a particularly sensitive assignment and was being withheld until just the proper moment. Treek wanted to believe this, but he just wasn't certain.

There was a sudden twinge at the corner of his mind,

and Treek easily shifted his concentration from his studies.

*"Attention, Treek, I have a thought-message from Commander Landor."* He recognized the sender as the deputy commander's assistant, Viadah. *"Shall I process it through now?"*

*"Yes. Please do."* This was it, he told himself. This was the beginning of the career he had been awaiting for decades. His assignment was at last about to be announced. But it seemed like eons before the actual message began.

*"We are pleased with the work you have done as part of the accelerated planetary survey program. Your duty assignment is now being processed and will be delivered to you immediately following the graduation exercises. You will be expected to report immediately for duty at that time. Therefore, we are canceling your last two days of work here and granting you a leave period during which you may wish to make any farewells to family and friends you deem necessary."*

The commander's message went on to detail the exact time of his return and other general information. However, Treek was not concentrating on the message. This was *not* his assignment. Why were they waiting? Didn't they have his assignment ready? Why make him wait any longer to find out what it was? And the message from the deputy commander seemed so cool and removed, almost as if it were designed for — and Treek realized this must be the case — many of his fellow classmates as well. It was not a personalized statement, at all. Somehow, this seemed to disturb Treek almost as much as the fact that he still had not received his duty assignment.

Finally, his mind slipped on to the other part of the message, the saying of "goodbyes." He must catch the first available planetary craft to Hulmar to be with

Dejung. But even before that, he knew there were two others whose minds he must touch.

His mind began to probe outward — searching. It had been a long time, too long. He had not allowed them to enter his head since that night months ago when he had revealed his intention to enter the survey program. Now that his dream was about to become reality, he missed them very much. He almost wished that he wouldn't be going, but he suppressed his urge to remain and rejoin Guin and Pera in the alliance of minds they had shared. His mind continued to grope outward, still searching, but he could not locate even the fringes of their closed minds. He sat motionless for almost an hour with his mind totally absorbed in the search. Slowly, one by one, he began to eliminate the possibilities. Their minds were not closed because then he could have detected the fringes of their thoughts. Nor were they dreaming, because he would have been able to enter their dream worlds and experience their fantaties. The same was true for "simulating." If they were in the long sleep, their mental activity would be so slow it would be almost undetectable, but they would hardly have elected suspended animation at this stage in their lives. Other possibilities seemed just as remote and ridiculous. Eventually he had eliminated all but two, and one of these seemed too ghastly to conceive. That they were both dead seemed very unlikely, however. So this left only one real possibility.

He didn't want to and he couldn't bring himself to accept this conclusion either, but he must check it out. Almost frantically now, his mind began to probe outward once again. This time he was reaching for the mind of Jone, Pera's parent. He would surely have the answer to this question.

*"Treek?"* came back the response from 20,000 miles away.

*"Oh, yes. Pera's friend. But he said you had broken off all contact, that you were in training for some special program. I'm sure he will be quite happy to receive your thoughts again."*

*"Yes, as I will be to touch his mind. I've been searching for both Pera and Guin. Can you tell me where either is?"*

*"Gone. They're both gone. They left together a week ago on an outing to Basidine III. They're cut off from communication there, but they should be back in a few days."*

Then it was true. He had missed them. There would be no contact.

*"Do you know when they will return?"*

There was no response from Jone for some time. Finally, an answer came back. *"No, no. I can't tell you for certain. It could be any day now, but there was no exact return date. Is that important?"*

*"I'm leaving Laazed on a mission in about three days. I may be gone for many decades, even centuries. I just wanted to contact them before I left. Would you please tell them — ?"*

*"To contact you when they return? Certainly!"* There was another pause, then Jone continued with much compassion. *"I'm sorry, Treek."*

A few hours later, Dejung, Taw, Carris, and Lozar welcomed him back to Hulmar, and even Taw wished him well in his new venture. But Treek could not fully concentrate on their activity. He was still yearning for Pera and Guin. Why, he asked himself, could mental energy reach more than 30,000 miles to span Laazed in the blinking of an eye but not penetrate the void of space? His friends were out there only four days journey away, but they were beyond his reach, perhaps forever. He was the one who had shunned them, and now they were unreachable when he needed them. He did not want to climb into an interplanetary craft three or four

days from now without touching their minds just once
more.

But that is what he did.

**Part II**

**GLORY'S FALL**

## CHAPTER EIGHT

He was on a command transport heading away from Laazed, three weeks out, nearing rendezvous with a two-person Scanner.

Treek still found it hard to believe that he could be working this far off the primary space channels and on such an insignificant assignment. Most of his classmates had long ago made their rendezvous and were by now on duty. Only three others besides Treek remained on board the transport which was plunging outward toward the galactic edge. Here, in a few short hours, Treek was to meet and relieve the first officer of the Scanner Holingar.

"First officer" seemed a rather pretentious title for the secondary surveyor on a two-person vessel. It was simply an attempt by the upper echelon to make an otherwise drab position seem more palatable. But it didn't. At least, not to him. There was still hope of getting out of here — after all, the Holingar's current "first officer" was accomplishing that feat, but at what price and how long had he served on the craft? Treek knew he could resign his commission and return to Laazed at any time, but that would put a damper on all his plans. He was certain his work out here would be nothing like the glamorous life Zokken had delighted him with in all those stories.

He sat in his chamber staring at the stars as they

appeared on his port window projection. Those
twinkling objects had beckoned him for more than half
his lifetime. But they looked very different out here.
Laazed's sun was no longer even visible. It was a
strange and vacant sky. The concentration of the few
nearby stars was certainly nothing to compare with
what he had known all his life on a world near the
galactic core. He almost felt as if he were being exiled to
some nether dimension beyond all he had known.

A buzzer sounded on the wall of the sparsely filled
room he had been occupying for the three weeks, and
Treek turned his attention away from the portal.

"Yes?" he asked in the formal, spoken language. It
was used in most official intra-ship communications.

"We have reached your rendezvous point. The other
vessel has not arrived, so we will hover here until
contact is made. It should be here shortly, according to
the last communication we had from the captain.
Therefore, you should report, with your belongings, to
the disembarkation chamber as soon as possible.

"Thank you. I shall," he replied, signing off. He knew
that "as soon as possible" meant "immediately."

Most of his "belongings" were in the chamber already.
Treek quickly moved around this room picking up the
few remaining items and stuffing them into a carry bag.
In moments, he too was riding the intra-ship tram to
the chamber.

As he sat in the disembarkation chamber waiting for
the small ship to dock, he thought about the two friends
whom he had been unable to contact. He wondered
what Guin and Pera had thought and felt when they
heard from Jone that he had sought them. Perhaps they
had been right about waiting, after all. In
a little over seven years he would have eligible for an
internship in the explorer program. But there was no
changing the past, he knew. They were gone from his

life and so was his chance to choose. He must now go forward in the direction he had taken. He would simply have to distinguish himself in the Survey Corps. He could still write his own ticket out of here. He wondered if that was what the Holingar's current first officer had done. Perhaps it was, but Treek didn't know. All he knew was that was what its new first officer planned to do.

The scanner was coming in. It had reported its position to the transport, and Treek had watched as it came into visual range and slowed its speed, gliding quietly through the void of space to its appointed docking bay. Seconds after the maneuver was complete, the bay doors slid open, and a tall, slender, tan-complected Laazene in Survey Corp dress crossed the threshold. His first officer insignia and other uniform markings were identical to the ones Treek wore.

"Gakhia," he said orally, identifying himself as he approached Treek. "I assume you are my replacement?"

Treek indicated assent with a downward motion of his right hand, then added, "I'm Treek."

Gakhia stopped momentarily, facing Treek. "The job's all yours. Good luck." Then he turned and walked from the room.

Treek stared in his direction for a few seconds. What had he meant by that remark? Was it simply a universal gesture of goodwill or was it something more?

Slowly he shifted his gaze back to the bay doors and began to walk toward the small craft docked there.

"*Welcome,*" said a voice inside his mind the moment he entered the craft. "*I'm Jecke, the 'captain' of this ship. You'll find me on the main deck. Please come up and join me.*"

Treek was relieved at least that Jecke wasn't using the formal spoken jargon that had been the rule in his life for the past three weeks while he was encapsulated in transit.

Quickly he moved completely inside as the door slid closed behind him. His belongings had already been loaded aboard by robot hands.

*"Yes, captain, I'm on my way."* And there was a flush of excitement in his thoughts. It might be small, but this was his first assignment.

## CHAPTER NINE

The Holingar's control room looked much as he had expected it would. During his accelerated training program, he had studied all the various craft that were utilized by the Survey Corps fleet. The only major difference in this vessel and the models he had studied was the R-Drive panel. The Scanner Holingar — on which he was now "second in command" — had a rather dated panel unit, but Treek guessed the Corps hardly made a great effort to put the latest equipment in operation this far out.

Jecke was going over the full range of instruments, a rather needless operation, Treek felt, since the ship required little of his broad knowledge. In the back chambers of his mind, Treek was taking mental note of his "captain." Jecke appeared somewhat shorter than Treek's nine-foot heighth and his ashen skin belied the fact that he was no junior corpsman. He was at least twenty-five hundred, Treek guessed, maybe as much as three thousand. The intensity level of his thought projection was powerful, as if he had long ago mastered the full range of his mind. His attitude seemed courteous, yet businesslike. Treek got the feeling that he had seen many "junior officers" come and go over the centuries. Suddenly there was harshness in the other's thoughts, and Treek realized Jecke was asking for a response.

"*Well? Didn't you understand me? Do you have any questions?*" he asked urgently.

Treek mentally composed himself. "*Yes! I mean: No! Not now.  But I'll probably have some soon — when we go into operation.*"

Jecke gave him a somewhat disturbing look, then moved on to another subject. Treek paid more attention this time.

"*We have eight planets in three systems that must be examined in the next three weeks, so it should be a fairly busy time. We'll work together closely during the first phase of your stint.*" There was emphasis on the last word, as if Jecke were getting weary of training associates. "*If you DO have questions, you should try to ask them then. After an initial period of training — of work — we'll move into areas where we can function independently.*"

Jecke's thought-projections trailed off as he turned his attention to the control of the ship. Since they had left the docking position with the transport, the Holingar had been on automatic control. Now Jecke moved to check the computer reports of stellar activity.

Treek's eyes surveyed the small compartment once more, and he moved to take the "first officer's" chair. Jecke had indicated his area of operation during the "initial period" of his duty on the Holingar, adding that eventually he would be "trained" in the control operation of the vessel also. Treek had submerged a mental grin at this thought, for he was certain he could handle a craft twice the size of this one without a single moment of additional instruction from his "captain."

On one level, time seemed to slip by very slowly for Treek, for, although he was now a "professional," he hardly felt fulfilled, but as the days and weeks passed, he kept very busy doing what duty as a stellar surveyor called on him to do. In two months, he had visited more planets than in all the rest of his lifetime. And these seemed to be an endless variety, all sizes and composition. Some had thriving plant and animal life, while others had only plants and still others were devoid of life altogether. Treek detested his work on these, for he was possessed of an eerie feeling of foreboding and doom every time he set foot on such barren rocks. He understood why he felt as he did about such planets, but that did little to relieve his anxiety. The psychological disturbance had occurred as a result of their visit to Demotav VI, one of the planets he had surveyed near the end of his first month with the Holingar.

He and Jecke had been working on separate parts of the planet, several hundred miles apart when Treek first noticed the unusual readings of his instruments. His mental alarm was immediately detected by Jecke because of his partner's alert mental perceptiveness.

"*What is it?*" he demanded.

"*I don't know. It's just that I'm getting impossible readings. Must be an instrument malfunction,*" Treek replied, trying to bring his sense of alarm under control.

"*Not likely. That scan unit has been adjusted for 99.999 per cent accuracy. I've never known its type to fail. There must be some other explanation. What is the reading?*"

"*Life! Carbon-based life!*" But there was nothing alive here, at least not carbon-based. With these levels of radioactivity, carbon life would be destroyed in a matter of seconds. They had been so certain of this that they had not dared set foot on this world without the extreme protection of the Aura. The Outer Skin could have protected them against the dangers of radioactivity, but if it were torn or otherwise damaged, death would have been instantaneous for the mind as well as the body. The Aura was much more cumbersome to use, but the protection from external damage was almost complete.

*"Are you certain you're not just misreading the scan unit?"* Jecke demanded. *"There isn't any life here."* Treek buried his anger deep under a mental facade, but his feeling of hurt and frustration was very real. This wasn't the first time Jecke had questioned his ability. How would he ever be able to get out of this assignment with the kind of rating he'd need to go into exploratory work if his superior questioned everything he did?

Quickly he examined the unit again. There was no question about the reading. The carbon combination he was getting could mean only one thing: life.

*"Perhaps you had better read those to me. Maybe I can help interpret them,"* Jecke thoughtsaid.

After an awkward pause of several seconds, Treek began to project the readings to the other. With difficulty he was holding back his emotion. What could Jecke hope to get from these readings that he had not "interpreted" already?

After he had finished with the readings, there was another brief pause before Jecke responded, and then it wasn't really a response to the readings at all.

*"Why don't you complete all your other tests and we'll meet in the Parent and discuss our findings."*

Treek rushed to finish his work and then climbed aboard his tiny one-person bio-sampler scout ship and piloted it hurriedly back to the Holingar. He had never adopted Jecke's use of the term "Parent" for the Holingar. It just seemed much too small itself to be the parent of anything.

He arrived long before Jecke and sat around the control room, nervously manipulating some of the minor control switches. When the other did arrive, he seemed in no hurry to discuss Treek's findings. Finally the junior officer could wait no longer and broached the subject himself.

Treek stared out at the viewscreen focused on the barren world below. He had the feeling a billion invisible eyes were watching his every move, tapping into his every thought. He was visibly shaken, and he was making little effort now to hide it from Jecke. *"What do you make of those readings? They DO mean life! Life is present on that planet. But how? And where?"*

His superior did not reply immediately, but he too stared at the viewscreen. For the first time, Treek realized that Jecke was considerably disturbed over something also.

Finally his thoughts came seeping into Treek's mind. *"No, life is not present there. Not now. But life was present on that world once a long time ago. I couldn't expect you to understand it or be prepared to interpret those readings. I can hardly accept it myself. But something like this happened to me once before."* He turned to look Treek full in the eyes. *"I was young then myself. Still a cadet, not much older than you. I was serving aboard the Wendka, and we were surveying a barren world just like this one."* He nodded toward the viewscreen. *"It too was radioactive. But that doesn't prove much. There's radioactivity all around us. Did you know that Laazed's antique spacecraft were atomic powered?"*

Treek motioned assent as Jecke paused again and seemed to brighten briefly with that last thought, then he continued in the same somber mood as before.

*"But we began to get those same life readings on that planet that you got here, and we were frightened and intrigued by the whole situation. We extended our stay there while we did more tests and looked for other signs of life around us. But there were none.*

*"Finally, by accident, we began to unearth the remains — the remains of a civilization which had thrived on that planet but which had destroyed itself! Destroyed not only*

*itself but every tiny bit of life on that planet many times over. It was horrible to conceive. That's why, when you told me there was life down there, I wanted your readings. I couldn't believe it had happened again. I thought and hoped there must be another explanation. But there isn't. I'm sure if we took time and started digging down there, somewhere we'd come up with bits of evidence of a civilization which destroyed itself and also its world."*

The thought was morbid, sickening. Treek couldn't imagine it — a civilization so twisted psychically that it could destroy everything which it held dear. Oh, he knew from his study of history that there had been many wars on Laazed, but that was *ancient history*. As civilized beings, his people had gone far beyond that. He couldn't understand how war and civilization could exist side-by-side, and here was disturbing evidence that they couldn't — not for long — without one destroying the other.

After that experience, Treek never visited a barren world without that gnawing feeling that he was being watched by the souls of countless dead. And even when there was little indication of radioactivity and no evidence of carbon life on these worlds, he was not reassured. He could envision death to many forms of life from many causes yet unknown to him and his kind.

He knew he should have felt reassured about Jecke's respect for his ability after hearing his companion's account. The other had made it clear that Treek could not have known about testing for the remains of life on an empty world. But still Treek felt there was some ill will between them because of his lack of experience, something which — if he had had it — might have given him a clue to solve the mystery of the evidence of life where there was no life. He could see clearly that he would have to take bold new strides if he were going to demonstrate his superior competence to Jecke and afterwards to the entire universe.

His opportunity came sooner than he expected.

## CHAPTER TEN

Treek's education as a stellar surveyor took a variety of twists and turns during the next few months.

He and Jecke visited Grachar VIII and found a wealth of mineral resources.

On Snanic II, they discovered a variety of animal life forming many levels of the evolutionary scale, all living in harmony. For some reason — which the explorers to follow them would try to find out — the planet contained no carnivores. Treek wished he were going to be among the members of that follow-up exploratory team, for his fascination with the planet's evolutionary development was greater than he had known for any other world they'd seen. He let his imagination run wild and pictured the planet in a few million years when intelligent life had developed — an intelligence which knew not war ever! It was an intriguing thought.

And then there was the Myam system which had to be quarantined because all the inhabitable planets were gripped by a deadly plague.

*"This IS strange. I've never seen anything like it,"* Jecke thoughtsaid. Then he added that he was always coming across things new to him. *"That's what keeps this business so fresh and alive. And I guess that's why I'd rather be a surveyor than anything else. Because we're the first. Sure, the explorers get to figure out the whys and the wherefores — but we're the first. We find*

*it; we report it; we set the pace."*

Treek had never thought of it that way. It gave him a clue to why Jecke had stayed out here at the edge of space for so many centuries. But it didn't change his own desire to be an explorer. He wanted more than to be the first. He wanted to find the answers to the questions they were posing.

*"How could it have happened?"* he asked. *"A whole system diseased and deadly. Climatically it's just perfect for our people. There must be at least three planets here that are habitable for Laazenes. But they're all infected. What could have caused it?"*

Jecke shrugged with a look of dismay. *"Could be anything. But it is curious. May be something in this sun's rays. Maybe a systemwide cloud spread disease from planet to planet. Maybe there were others who came here before us and carried this plague all around. (We've to reason to think we're the first.) We can't know. But we do know that the fact that these planets are inhabitable for us makes them even more dangerous. That's why we must quarantine the whole system."*

Treek did not question Jecke's logic. He just wanted to know more of the why. He couldn't understand it. Here Jecke seemed very excited by their unusual find — because they had found it. But he was content to leave the checking to the explorers — who might never even come to a quarantined system this far out. There were just too many other inhabitable planets closer to home. Where was Jecke's curiosity? The curiosity of the young surveyor who had been part of a team whose members couldn't be satisfied until they understood why there was no life on a dead planet which their instruments told them had life? Perhaps it was because of just such experiences that Jecke didn't want to check further here. He was secretly afraid of what they might find this time. Maybe that was why he was so well-suited to his work on the outer perimeter, Treek concluded. But these thoughts did little to satisfy Treek's curiosity.

The senior surveyor stared at his computer panels confirming their preliminary findings. Methodically, he punched up several more readings and included them in his master report. Treek studied his thoughts intensely, but most of Jecke's incredulity was, by now, gone. His mind was set on completing the job, not on their ominous findings. He had stopped transmitting his thoughts to Treek, but there was no effort to keep the junior member out of his head. There seldom was. Treek often marveled at the other's mental control and wondered how he could keep his mind so completely open and receptive and yet develop inner thoughts — for certainly he must have some that Treek could not read. Every person must, or face insanity. The psychologists had known that for generations. But somehow Jecke had so mastered his mind that he could maintain a surface receptiveness while holding secret thoughts. Treek had heard of mental masters who could do this, but he had never before known anyone who could.

He found himself in a quandary over this partner of his. Jecke was a simple person, dedicated only to doing his duty as a surveyor; yet, at the same time, he was a master of ultimate mental skill and control. Treek doubted Jecke would have had any trouble getting transferred to any Survey Corps assignment anywhere in the galaxy. He was certain Jecke could perform far above the competency level in whatever he was called upon to do. But his companion seemed content to continue his work on the edge of space decade-after-decade, century-after-century. Treek envied the other's contentment — something he could never share.

Jecke finally completed his computations and swiveled his seat around to face Treek. Effortlessly, he pulled his eight-foot frame to a standing position, his ashen skin glistening. Gradually a glow of satisfaction spread across his long, slender face. He looked his companion full in the eyes.

*"Our work here is finished, my friend,"* he thoughtsaid. *"We have nothing more to do. I've filed the report with central, and I've punched up our next destination."*

As if he were collecting his thoughts, he paused momentarily. *"Treek"* — he seldom addressed his companion by name since there were only the two of them on board — *"I know you'd like to find answers to these and other questions, but that is not our job. We must go elsewhere and do what is required of us there. We have many counting on us. If we don't go on, we'll fall behind and make it difficult for the exploratory teams set to follow us. Besides, we don't have the equipment, training, or personnel to accomplish a follow up. I'm sorry."*

Had he been that easy to read? Treek wondered.

*"I must take a rest period now. I'd like you to take over the controls, guide us into the next system, then take the prelims,"* Jecke concluded.

Why was he doing this? Auto could do it all except the prelims. Was the captain simply trying to soothe him, to pacify him? Treek was uncertain. He knew he should be delighted with this, his very first opportunity to solo, but he found himself somehow feeling suspicious and put upon.

Jecke left the control compartment without further statement, and immediately Treek slammed the door to his mind.

Slowly, with a mixture of elation and confusion, Treek slipped into the command chair normally occupied by the "captain." He slid his twelve slender, brown fingers back and forth along the arms of Jecke's chair.

Command was his now. He was in control of the
Holingar. It would go where he sent it. If he chose, he
could deviate from the prescribed course punched in by
Jecke. He could turn the vehicle and send it
plummeting toward the center of the galaxy and Laazed.
Something in a corner of his brain urged him to do just
that. It told him that he was wasting his time here, that
he would never be fulfilled as long as he skimmed the
perimeters of the galaxy in such an insignificant vessel.
There was excitement and promise out there, but he
would never find it as long as he accepted this — this
*exile*! His hands reached out to shift the ship's position
and send it scurrying away from this nothingness.

Then abruptly three faces popped into memory:
Zokken, who had given him a goal; and Pera and Guin,
who had befriended him and urged him not to make
this move to begin with. But none of them would have
wanted what he was contemplating. Treek realized that
neither would he. Instantly, he jerked his hands away
from the control panel.

For hours he sat in the command chair, mechanically
going through the motions of control.

The ship glided at last into the fringes of the system
Jecke had punched in. The Holingar's first officer
rushed into action, slowing the ship to sublight and
sending out instrument scans in the directions of the
eight significant planets indicated by the computer.

After hours of mind-numbing nothingness, this was a
time of action. Treek slowed the ship further and began
to interpret the readouts on each of the planets. Two of
the worlds, the fifth and the sixth, were giants, with one
of them an astronomical oddity: a "ringed" planet. The
other giant also had rings, though they were too small
to qualify it officially for that category. But neither of
these giants showed any indication of life forms. Nor
was there much possibility of carbon-based life on the

outer planets, which were much too far from this moderate-sized sun for sufficient heat to support normal development. There were some interesting mineral possibilities on these, however, especially the seventh and eighth, both of which were slightly larger than Laazed. There was also a ninth world, a planetoid actually, that was very small, barren and frozen on the far edge of this solar system. Scanning inward, Treek found that the second, third, and fourth planets were the best possibilities for life development because of their distances from this sun. The first planet was small, though larger than the planetoid at the other end of the system, and it was also too close to the solar body to be inhabitable by his people.

For now, Treek focused his attention on those worlds most likely to support life. There was clearly no indication of life on the fourth and little prospect for the second. But the third seemed right. All the conditions were conducive. There definitely should be life there and in abundance!

A broad smile jumped onto Treek's lips, and he quickly laid in a course to the third planet. Jecke would certainly want to check it out first. He was so excited about his find that he punched up the maximum safe speed on the Holingar's computers. In a matter of moments, the ship swung into orbit around the modest-sized planet. During the course of those moments, he had stayed busy making other prelims: temperature, atmosphere, planetary density. There was much which his instruments could tell him even from far out.

Now Treek ran through all the orbital tests quickly. In less than an hour after swinging into orbit around this system's third planet, he had checked readouts in all the major test areas. The rest would have to wait for landing.

Waiting, however, was not one of Treek's favorite

occupations. He quickly scanned all the major tests again. Yes, definitely this world was swarming with habitation, both plant and animal. The nitrogen/oxygen atmospheric composition appeared toxic to Laazenes, but if his people wished to live on this world for any extended time, they could easily modify their metabolism to accept it. The planet's diameter was approximately one-third that of Laazed and its density closer to one-fourth, but the milder gravity should prove no problem to his people. Because of its orbital pattern and rotation, however, its years and days were both surprisingly similar in length to those known on Laazed.

For some reason, this planet held a strange attraction to Treek. He was aware of this, but he could not figure why. In the several months he had served aboard the Holingar, he had visited many inhabited worlds. But none had held the attraction of this one. Perhaps it was simply because he had found it himself. It was his discovery alone, with no help from Jecke. Now he could hardly wait for his superior to awaken so they might visit its soil.

But Jecke might continue sleeping for hours. And, after all, this was his find. Why shouldn't he make the first visit alone? There was no regulation against it. This just might be the first step toward that glorious future which had thus far eluded him. When Jecke saw his initiative, the captain was bound to commend him. And the more he thought about the possibility of making the initial visit alone, the more he liked it. This was his world, his find. But in the back of his mind, there was still a twinge of fear which he could not allay completely.

Still, somehow he was not ready to leave the Holingar in his one-person bio-sampler. Carefully, he studied each of the readouts, then flipped on the monitor of Jecke's chamber. The other was sleeping soundly, so soundly that Treek reasoned he might even be back aboard the Holingar before Jecke awakened.

Suddenly it was settled. He still had flirting doubts, but he tucked them away. He must hurry. More than anything else, he now wanted to make his departure before Jecke awoke. And the thought of returning before his companion arose also held much appeal. He might just pull it off, he reasoned, if he hurried. The more he thought about it, the more excited he became. This was his world awaiting below, and he must be the first Laazene to set foot on its soil.

Moving quickly in his excitement, Treek hastily flipped all the Holingar's controls on autopilot and scurried below to the bio-sampler scout bay where the two tiny craft were housed. He was confident that if anything went wrong aboard the Holingar, its master computer would sound the alarm and awaken Jecke. But there should be no problem.

Hurriedly, he climbed into the scout and secured himself only seconds before the hangar door opened, responding to his earlier command. The small scout's simple control panel easily responded to his excited hand movements, and he was plunging toward the planet almost immediately.

He felt so much closer to the stars now in this small ship, with its clear, oval roof and its single chamber, hardly large enough to support one individual even in a sitting position. Peeking over the rim of the planet was this system's brilliant yellow sun; this world's lone moon loomed close by, over his left shoulder. It was the stuff Laazed's poets had written about millennia ago.

Then he was breaking through the world's dense cloud mass and closing fast on brilliant green foliage and vast, sparkling blue oceans. It was beautiful, looking peaceful and untouched from his vantage point. The glow of his excitement darkened his skin tone to a deep brown as a fleeting thought of Zokken fluttered through his mind.

Treek knew at last he was coming into his own.

## CHAPTER ELEVEN

Treek halted the scout's vertical drop and pushed it into horizontal motion, avoiding a landing in the midst of an immense body of water. He skimmed low over the planet, only a few thousand feet in the air. With his naked eyes, he could easily make out details of the world below. Once he reached the periphery of a land mass, he let the craft drop even lower and continued to skim. Now he could make out individual creatures — and they were many and varied — but nowhere was there indication of advanced civilization. There were some primitive, biped semi-beasts hunting in packs. In maybe a million years or so these might develop into civilized creatures, but there was also an equal chance that they would not.

So this was Treek's world.

Abruptly, he slowed the tiny craft's forward motion and dropped quietly downward toward a clearing of meadow land. Here was a lush world. The clearing was a lustrous green, with many small fauna samples scampering among the plantlife. He had examined many worlds similar to this one in the time he had served with Jecke. Still, there was something about this planet which intrigued his senses more than normal. Had the compulsion that drew him here grown out of his hunger for discovery alone, or was there something more? From orbit, this had appeared to be a water world, blue and enswirled with layers of dense clouds hiding much of the land mass. But his instruments had indicated this land and life below. It was, of course, a young world by galactic standards; however, there was a great beauty here that seemed to beckon him to some unknown destiny.

He stepped gingerly from the scout, wearing a simple Outer Skin over his nine-foot frame. He saw little need to slip into the more cumbersome Aura for the few surface tests he planned to make. Though this world seemed quite simple, it appeared biologically stable, inhabited by a vast array of creatures, but none mentally developed. He felt confident that he could be finished with his sampling and docked in "Mother" long before Jecke completed his rest period.

Several small creatures with bushy tails and reddish-brown fur ran past him as he set about matter-of-factly placing mineral and soil test units throughout the meadow and surrounding woodland. Familiarity with his work had helped him overcome the anxiety he felt when he had first visited worlds like this. Consequently, he took little note of a swift movement in the bushes less than a dozen footsteps ahead of him — a movement so simple, yet one which would radically alter his existence.

"Ay-e-e-e-e-e!"

His thoughtscream fell vacant in the mental void of the jungle planet. The sudden burst of pain in his abdomen was excruciating.

A crude wood and stone spear protruded from his midsection, near his middle breather. He realized immediately that even if his lung didn't collapse, he might soon die from the deadly gases entering through the rupture in the Skin.

"Jecke!" he thoughtshouted in agony, his desperation blurring his knowledge that there was no hope of summoning his companion. The atmosphereless void of space presented a barrier that no telepathic thought could penetrate.

But Jecke would come soon when he found him missing. He'd trace him down, Treek told himself.

Color was draining from his ripple-textured, brown body. His strength was quickly slipping away as the poison oozed throughout his system. He was even having trouble focusing his attention on the situation. A new conglomeration of thoughts and emotions — from fear to elation — danced lightly through his head.

Suddenly, in his mind, he was back home on Laazed. He was a youth again, dreaming of becoming a stellar explorer like Zokken. But his companions, Guin and Pera, were waging a thought-battle within his brain. He felt like a spectator as their telepathic thoughts swirled like a vortex.

He could not hold these thoughts either, however, and soon they too slipped away. Once again, he realized he was on the jungle planet and that in the distance something was approaching. A compulsion, just at the level of consciousness, urged him to fight back, but, try as he might, he could not bring his surroundings into sharp focus. He stumbled backwards, sprawling over a small sapling. The thud of his own impact brought him more fully back to reality. He could now see — advancing toward him — a cluster of the hairy, primitive bipeds. They were carrying crude wood and stone weapons and appeared to be closing in for the kill.

*"Beasts!"* he thoughtscreamed.

The statement was a mixture of the anger, frustration, and despair inside him. If he could only reach the scout, he could stop them. But his strength was gone, sapped by his injury and the poison spreading inside his body. How stupid he'd been to come alone to this desolate world.

Gradually, he could feel the darkness closing in around him, and he realized that the poison atmosphere might rob these savages of the glory of their kill. A large group had now emerged from the cover of the trees and were circling him.

Faintly, he could see a smaller but vicious-looking furry creature hiding in the nearby underbrush, and he had a glimmer of hope where seconds before there had been none. Further, his frenzied mind told him, it could be a possible instrument for his revenge. Even now as he lay sprawled upon this alien soil — dying — he knew there were dangers in this unknown path. But he reasoned they could be no worse than the certain death which would overtake him in seconds if he did not act. This conclusion he would later challenge thousands of times.

He closed out reality, deliberately absorbing the blackness of limbo. Rallying his fading energy, he thrust the electrical impulses forming his mind outward toward the simple and frightened small beast. When he let the web of darkness clear from his thoughts, he found himself in strange surroundings, and he was certain the teletransference had been completed — that his mind now had a new home!

From his lowly position in the small beast's body, Treek could see the primitives now attacking his own dead form with clubs, and the fury began to swell inside him. Gone were the millennia of control which had kept the Laazene primeval capacity for violence in check. He felt hatred flush within him and some new, previously unknown feelings as well. He was gripped by an overwhelming desire to chew these primitives to bits. He realized then that he did not have complete control over the small creature in which he had housed his mind. He tried, with much effort, to bring his emotions under control, but he could not. He knew there must be some secret to complete dominance of the host mind, but he could not remember what his teachers had said.

As he stared through weak, blurry eyes at the slaughter but a short distance from him, he could contain himself no longer. The mutilated form being destroyed only a few feet away was his own body. Angrily now, he pushed his host forward, bounding blindly toward the cluster of ragged hunters. He drew the beast's lips upward in a vicious snarl just before his mouth made contact with a leg of the nearest primitive. He caught the biped off guard with his charge and knocked it to the ground. Instinctively he lunged for the other's throat, but the primitive fought back fiercely, flaying at its tormentor with its upper limbs. He tried desperately to reach his appointed target, but the savage continued to jab with its upper limbs, bringing blow after blow down upon his head. Treek felt a painful throbbing beginning around his host's eyes, but he kept pushing the small beast's body forward, again and again trying to reach the biped's throat. All the while his adversary was scrambling backwards, pushing itself along with movements of its shoulders and lower limbs. The struggle between them seemed almost a stalemate, with Treek nipping the skin of the other's hands and the primitive landing fleeting blows on the body and head of Treek's smaller host form. The struggle might have gone on like this indefinitely had not another of the bipeds taken note of the battle and intervened.

Treek first realized he had a second adversary when he felt the point of a spear prick his back. He glanced around only in time to see a large stone come crashing down on his neck. The blow crushed Treek's offensive, and he fell back, away from his first target.

He felt blood spurting from his wounds, and the meadow and its primitive occupants seemed to be dashing by him in a maddening spin. Quickly, he turned his host's feet to flee, but he felt a shower of smaller stones pounding his body. It was evident that several of the savages had turned on him. He made a frantic dash for the underbrush from which he had emerged moments earlier, knowing the larger animals would have trouble reaching him there.

And just as he reached sanctuary, all went black again.

## CHAPTER TWELVE

He saw images of weird jungle creatures.

The smell of rotting flesh brought beads of saliva to the tip of his tongue.

He was being chased by a giant, furry, brown creature along a winding jungle trail. It was gaining on him. He could hear its fierce roar and feel its hot, nauseating breath on his neck. Then he saw a small hole at the base of a large tree, and he made a lunge for it. Just as he ducked his tail inside, he felt vicious claws rake him. But he knew he was safe. The ugly claw reached inward to strike him again, but it could not stretch far enough to touch him. He sat quietly now, panting.

Strangely, Treek knew he was dreaming, but the images looked all too familiar to him. It was as if a part of him accepted it, while the other part was mystified.

Gradually, painfully, he opened strange eyelids.

These were not his eyes, Treek knew. Then he must still be dreaming. But he knew he wasn't.

He felt sharp and throbbing pain in his head.

He also felt fur growing from his pores. This could not be his body. What kind of uncanny tricks was his mind playing on him?

He was lying in a pool of blood in a rancid pile of dead and decaying leaves. But where was his bunk?

There was something vaguely familiar in the distance,

but he was having trouble focusing on it. These eyes were weak and coated with a crust of blood and other body secretions.

He sent a message to his back legs to — hold it! Back legs? What back legs? As a biped, he had only two legs! Why would he think of them in terms of "back legs"? But it did seem natural. Anyway, they would not respond to his message. They refused to move.

Part of him wanted to believe that he was having some wild, unbelievable nightmare, but another part told him to lick his bloody left front paw.

He could not understand what was happening, yet it all seemed natural and right at the same time!

Except for the pain and the failure of his body to respond to his mind's commands. He could move his head and neck but nothing below it would budge.

He rubbed his eyes on his right forelimb and squinted at the hazy object in the distance. His vision was still blurry and the thunder inside his head would not cease, but gradually the object became recognizable. It was his bio-sampler scout, and it was setting in the midst of a brilliantly green meadow. But what was it doing there with its exit ramp dangling open? And why was he here?

He stared down at the coarse, gray hair that covered his forelimbs and the heavily padded paw at their tips. Suddenly a flicker of memory shot through his mind. Then more and more of it came back to him: his mind, his essence, his very being was now housed in the body of a small, hairy beast. That explained why so many of his thoughts seemed both strange and normal at the same time: the creature's mind was struggling for dominance of its body. He should easily have been able to subdue the alien thought patterns, but perhaps the ordeal of transference had weakened his mental ability. That and the battle his host body had waged with the savages. The battle — of course! That was it; that was why he was here. That was why he could...not...move the creature's limbs. He was paralyzed!

From the underbrush where he had taken refuge, he now peered out at the scene of the recent struggle. The hairy primitives were all gone, but so was own natural body. The savages must have taken it away for a meal. With the disappearance of his original form, so went his hopes for revitalization in his natural body. It was a sobering thought. The nine-foot frame which had been the home for his being throughout all his 73 years was now gone, dead, and probably eaten. He knew it had been thoroughly smashed by the savages; he had seen them pounding it again and again with heavy, wooden clubs. Again, there was a flush of anger and hatred running through his thoughts, and he knew the creature's mind was affecting his. He fought for complete dominance once again, realizing that he must make his escape from this creature's body soon or their minds would become inseparably mingled. He wondered how much longer he had before he became part Laazene and part alien beast, but he knew there was no easy answer to that question. It all depended upon one's mental strength, and he realized his was largely untested. He knew that someone like Jecke could probably go on perhaps for days or weeks asserting himself, holding off the mingling of minds, but Treek knew he could never hold out that long.

With his thoughts of Jecke, his hope was renewed. Why must mental energy be limited to movement around bodies with large gravitational pull? Why couldn't it break away and seep through the void of space? Oh, sure, he told himself, he knew all the scientific reasoning behind it, but that didn't help him at this moment.

Yes, there was still hope for him. He knew that when Jecke found him missing with the scout, and after he did not return in a reasonable period, his companion would surely trace the small vessel down. He knew that his people could provide him with a cultivated, mindless biode — an exact genetic duplicate of his original body — to house his mental energy. Now, he must simply wait for Jecke to come to his rescue, as he knew his captain surely must.

The thunderbolts inside his head now crashed louder and stronger. The throbbing of his neck muscles also seemed more pronounced. If he had been able to feel the muscles in the rest of the creature's body, he was certain the pain would be excruciating. Perhaps the paralysis was almost a blessing. He tried to mask the pain in thoughts of far-off Laazed, but abruptly the curtain of unconsciousness fell again.

More dreams now. However, they weren't all bad. Most were a mixture of what he had known on his home planet and what this creature had known. Some would even have amused him — at another time and another place.

Now something was calling him back. But he was not ready to give up his dream world. He fought against it, resisting the call to awaken. Finally, his unconsciousness gave in, and Treek opened the creature's crusty eyes to peer out at this alien world again. What he saw, however, was not alien, but familiar.

His mind screamed a cry of relief.

*"Jecke!"* He flung his thoughts outward.

There, but a short distance from him, was his companion examining the scene of the battle.

*"I'm over here, Jecke, in this underbrush. I'm alive; my mind is alive! I've saved my mind. It's here, housed in the body of a small creature. Here — over HERE!"*

But Jecke did not stir from his position.

*"PLEASE, Jecke! Help me! I can't move! This beast's*

*injured. I'm paralyzed. Over here!"*

Still, there was no response.

Now Treek began to panic. Why wasn't Jecke responding to him? Surely his senior couldn't be that angry.

Quickly he surveyed his own situation again. His natural body destroyed by the savages, he was sharing the body of a smaller, simple-minded creature which had been wounded — perhaps mortally — in a battle with the savages. Now Jeeke had come for him, but somehow his captain was not responding to his messages of distress.

Then slowly there was another dawning as he ferreted out more bits of information from the vast amount of training he had received at Deame.

*"No! No! Jecke! Help me! HELP ME!"* he pleaded.

But there was still no sign from the other that he was even conscious of Treek's presence.

Gradually, Treek began to accept what must be the ghastly truth. It had been one of the risks in any teletransference effort: Even if a creature's neural system were advanced enough to host the mental processes of an intelligent being, often it lacked the corresponding mental transmission power to allow that mind to communicate telepathically with another. More importantly, there was an even more grisly probability: Without telepathic powers, another teletransference was impossible unless there was outside aid in achieving the process. The reality that Treek now felt was a far cry from those cold, intellectually isolated discussions he had known in Namar's mental control class.

Giving up was not something Treek did readily, however. He tried desperately to fling his mind outward again, this time to share Jecke's body — but he could not.

*"Trapped! I've trapped myself!"* His thoughts would

have encircled this globe instantly, he knew, if his mind still inhabited his natural body, but then there would have been little need to cry out.

Belatedly, he realized the strain was draining the small beast's energy, but he refused to stop.

*"Jecke, please hear me. SAVE ME!"*

The continued effort was making him quite dizzy. He knew that if he did not relinquish his pressure on this beast's energy soon, he might bring about the death of them both.

Jecke was now checking the various tests which Treek had placed in the meadow, but he suddenly glanced toward the underbrush where Treek lay.

A new flicker of hope arose in the mass of aching and bleeding flesh that housed two far different beings, joined in a common bond of fear. Had he somehow gotten through to Jecke? Treek feared making another projection immediately, however, for he knew he was teetering just at the borderline between consciousness and unconsciousness — perhaps between life and death itself.

But Jecke was walking toward him! Had his captain's super brain turned up its level of receptiveness by some means? Would he be saved, after all?

He heard the snapping of small twigs beneath Jecke's feet and the rustling of leaves as the other drew nearer. Treek could even see that Jecke was encased in his Aura instead of an Outer Skin, as he had worn.

The older Laazene came closer and closer to where Treek lay. Now he was only a few feet away. Then he halted and turned instead toward the bio-sampler scout Treek had piloted.

*"No, Jecke. Stop! COME BACK! Please, come back!"*

One last time Jecke paused and looked in Treek's direction, as if he had picked up faint thought waves. Then Treek felt his companion's thoughts enter his mind.

"*I've searched for you, Treek, but the evidence says that you're dead, killed by some wild beast before you could save your body or that dynamic, inquisitive mind of yours. I know this must be true. But somehow I'm unable to accept it; I can almost feel your presence here, even as we felt a mental consciousness on that dead, radioactive world. I know it must be my affection for you which makes me hesitate.*" His thought-projection stopped abruptly, as if he were unwilling to complete what he had intended. Then, finally, as he stared toward the vacant craft before him, he added: "*Goodbye, Treek; I will not forget you.*"

And then he was gone.

## CHAPTER THIRTEEN

Green. All was green.

Treek now knew that green was the color of horror, the hue of dispair.

Green surrounding him everywhere. Lush, green foliage on the trees. Green grass.

And a green prison.

The world which only hours earlier he had thought of as "Treek's world" and as a lush, young planet of beauty had taken on the look of desolation. For here he was abandoned.

Jecke was gone! Beyond all hope, he was gone. Presumed dead by his superior, Treek had been abandoned. Not only that, but Jecke had taken the survey samples with him and had taken Treek's bio-sampler scout in tow — all back to the Holingar. Back to the "Parent" ship! That term always seemed strange as Jecke applied it, but not any more. The Holingar was indeed his parent in a very real sense. It was the source of his life and his hope for the future. Now, no doubt, it had even departed this system altogether.

Imprisonment in this nightmare of green would be bad enough, Treek reasoned, if he were his own natural self, but he was not. Instead, *he* was a small, stupid beast — a small, *dying,* stupid beast. Paralyzed and doomed to death by starvation, if not from the wounds which he had suffered. There was great pain in the upper portion of *his* being, the neck and head. The rest still had no feeling at all. Treek knew that it didn't have to be so, that he could will the body to death. But wasn't this suffering punishment for what he had done? Besides, he was not sure he had the courage to face the final curtain of darkness. His mind could still do many things, even imprisoned in the body of a beast. But his mind had put him where he was. It was, at once, both the villain that had destroyed all his hopes and the potential instrument for his salvation.

*"But it shall be nothing!"* he declared, determined to do nothing to affect his new body's chances for recovery. And gradually he withdrew control from the entity.

Now, a new and thoroughly alien consciousness emerged to assume authority over this form. Treek watched almost unconcernedly from a corner of the brain which housed his intellect.

A low, yet shrill whine came from his throat.

Oddly, too, the world smelled different. With each whiff of his nostrils, there came a variety of odors which were instantly decoded and broken down into categories: bitter, sweet, sour; squirrel, monkey, other dogs.

"Other dogs"? That category had a distinction. It was suddenly clear that this was what the creature perceived itself as — a "dog." That was his name for his kind.

"His"? That was another! That thought-phrase picked up from the dog's mental vocabulary felt similar to what Treek had always used, but there was a subtle difference. It was something he had given little thought before. Indeed, when had there been pause to consider such things? But now he knew. This creature was not like his kind in another important aspect: It was a "single-sexes." A monosexual. It could function as only half a parent. This seemed so strange to the detached

Treek, now unencumbered by the pain or other bodily distractions of the beast. He recalled his studies of this kind during his childhood days on Laazed. What he had learned had concerned him little back then. Now he was confronted with it. How unnatural it seemed not to be a complete, total parent. But this creature in which he now resided was only half, the male half. He could never know the total joy of parenthood as...as Dejung had! Treek suddenly felt deprived of a fundamental right.

His thoughts were brought around to more immediate concerns as the creature continued to sniff the air. Registering on its brain cells was a new category of smells, all classified, more or less, as "disturbing" — tiger, bear, man. That last one brought on a mental frenzy. And once again, Treek had a flash of revelation. "Man" was the creature, the savage, pre-intelligent being which had damaged this "dog" in the recent fight. He was the enemy and was to be feared. But he was also a source of amazement for the dog, for he was like no other creature of the forest. He walked upright and carried things to bring pain to others, the most fearsome of which was the yellow, hot substance which danced around the jungle floor when released by man and which attacked everything in its path. When it had gone, everything was dead, not only dog, but bear, tiger, and even the silent giant: the tree. Nothing could withstand its burning, hot tongue — this "yellow tongue of death," the dogs called it.

And there was bewilderment in the mind of the dog — not because of his pain and agony; he could accept that. Even his paralysis was something to be accepted. But the strange and terrifying thoughts that had seized him and shown him "not real" places was frightening even more than the thought of the yellow tongue of death. It was something which could not be understood.

Treek knew the dog was taxing its mind beyond its

capacity at a time when physical injury was requiring much of the body's strength. Fortunately, the beast had a cutoff valve which activated itself when the strain became too great. Treek sensed that it was about to activate. And he was right. Mercifully, the curtain of unconsciousness fell again.

Oddly, his own consciousness was unaffected by this change. It gave him a queasy sensation unlike anything he had ever experienced before. He could not account for the phenomenon, only supposing it might be related to his effort to breakaway from control of the dog's physical form. Now he found himself a spectator in a strange menagerie of thoughts.

The dog had coupled its fear of man and other creatures of its domain, like the tiger and bear, with its apprehension about the strange thoughts inside its own mind, and these were forming into fantastic dreams of its own destruction. Mingled with it all was the flaming yellow tongue of death which was consuming everything in its path. Treek found this lower form's effort to cope with the unknown both fascinating and disturbing. But undermining what would have been the joy of experiencing reality from a totally new perspective was his own anxiety. Looming like a giant cloud over his every thought was the fact that he was a prisoner in an alien environment.

*"Was there ever such a prisoner?"* he asked himself, for there was no one else present to read his thoughts. And even if there had been, they could not have heard him. It was abundantly evident from Jecke's rescue attempt that this creature's base threshold for telepathy was far below the minimum level. Or was it? Perhaps its abilities were simply taxed and drained due to its physical injuries, injuries which he had caused. But if he had allowed harm to befall this body, he could also bring relief. He understood the principles of telekinetic

medicine, of self-healing; however, as a Laazene, he had never had to practice it consciously. Generations ago his people had so mastered their minds and bodies that the self-healing process became as automatic as breathing. Treek had simply never been conscious of it before. It was a function of his mind which was performed without his prior consent. Now, he sensed that he would have to give more than his consent for the process to begin on the body of this beast that housed his mind. He would have to work at it.

But he hesitated.

It was not something Treek wanted to do. If it were simply a healing of the dog, he would have gladly committed his mental energy to the task immediately, he assured himself. He had no desire to see any being in pain. But there was more, a prerequisite to the healing process. He knew of no other way. The mingling of minds was necessary for the process to be effective. They could no longer remain separate, for this time the mingling must be thorough, complete, irrevocable. There could be no turning back. Once it was done, no matter what body he inhabited, his mind would henceforth be part Laazene/part dog — part cultured and intelligent/part wild and simple. It was not an opportunity he rushed to embrace.

The dog was still unconscious, and, because of this, so was Treek's window on this world. Its external sensors were all but shut down: He could not see what was going on around him and the sounds and smells entering the brain were severely muffled. It was an unusual and sometimes terrifying predicament, being conscious in the corner of an unconscious mind. It heightened his realization that he was caged and trapped. He thought again of escape, the ultimate escape, but willing his own death was something which seemed even too ghastly to conceive. Treek felt torn among a conglomeration of frightening possibilities.

His indecision was foreshortened by fate.

Abruptly, the dog began to jerk and wheeze and gasp for breath, and Treek sensed that it was nearing its end unless he intervened.

Immediately his choice was made. Even a lifetime half beast/half person seemed desirable to death.

He flung his own consciousness into the midst of the dog's. Instantly he was enveloped in a frenzy of hysteria and wild delusions.

The bear was there, still chasing him, but instead of sharp, vicious claws, its greatest weapon was its tongue, the yellow tongue of death, which lashed out at Treek and burned the tip of his ears and his tail. The path on which he fled was made of flames, and the demon keeper of death — man — was blocking it with a club that he swung wildly as Treek approached. He saw that he could not leave the path, for tigers guarded it along all sides. Death was waiting for him in every direction.

But Treek fought with all the force of his mind to overcome these thoughts. Something — just at the edge of consciousness — told him to cling to hope, that death could be beaten; but he could not remember how.

Finally, he felt exhaustion, great exhaustion, overtaking him. He felt himself sinking down, down, down into a deep pit. There was only a dim remembering. He knew at last that this was the direction of hope, and he channeled the descent, guiding it into a deep and tranquil sleep. The fall continued; he seemed to be turning slowly as if he were in free-fall — end-over-end, falling forever.

The body was now in a deep trance. Breathing had slowed until it was almost undetectable. There was no consciousness of the outside world. And the dreams inside the body were now calm, soothing ones.

In the underbrush he lay, all but obscured from the

world of activity around him. The mind had spun its cocoon, and there would be no emergence until the body came forth renewed.

## CHAPTER FOURTEEN

Hunger.

That was his first sensation. Even before he opened his eyes, Treek felt an overwhelming emptiness.

He had no idea how long he had lain in the brush mending, but there seemed to be a nip in the air that he had not felt when he last had eyes opened on this world. How many rotations of this planet had that been? A week? A month? There was no way for him to tell.

All he wanted was to eat. A nice, juicy rabbit would taste good.

His tongue curled from his mouth and licked outward in anticipation of the feast.

No! Something was wrong. He didn't eat flesh. The thought of consuming another animal almost nauseated him.

He was trying to unravel this mystery when a clump of brown fur fell from a tree just a few feet from him, and he was upon it before the creature had time to scamper away. A few seconds later, he was again licking his lips, this time to savor the last few drops of blood which remained there.

The young squirrel had been a good appetizer, but he would have to partake of something more substantial if he were to stave off starvation.

He paused long enough to take account of his restored body. He felt weak from the long fast, but

everything seemed to be in good working order. He
thought of the synthesized meals he had known on the
Holingar, but the realization that he would probably
never taste another only served to make him more
hungry. There were plenty of rabbits around; they
would have to do. In fact, they would do nicely.

Taking a deep breath, he sampled the conglomeration
of odors surrounding him. There were no recent rabbit
smells, but a deer had passed this way not long ago. He
drooled at the thought of deer meat. What a feast that
would make! But those creatures were so swift and wily
they were almost impossible to catch, even when he was
in prime shape. In his weakened condition, he would be
no match for one. However, that didn't stop his
daydreaming about the feast.

He took another deep whiff of air. There was
something in it which hadn't been there before: man!
And the scent was getting stronger. The carrier of the
yellow tongue of death was coming toward the clearing.

The hair on the back of his neck stood on end. His
enemy was approaching. He must wait and take his
revenge. He would kill this savage.

He could hear the creature crashing through the
trees, and it made his mind chuckle. Man was so
clumsy. He didn't know how to hide his approach at all.
He always came crashing without regard for what lay in
his path. And the sickening smell of rotting skins which
he wore as well as his own offensive odor always gave
him away to any who cared to take heed.

Treek could see the smelly one emerging on the
opposite side of the clearing, but he was many — a
whole pack of man beings, it appeared. Slowly, the
Laazene/dog began to slink back toward the
underbrush where he had lain for so long. This did not
seem the time to seek his revenge. There were too many
of them, and they would stick together in a fight, even

as they had before. He would find the opportunity to avenge himself, but this wasn't it.

Quietly he began to crawl from the brush on the opposite side from the clearing, on the forest side. Once he had pulled himself free of entanglements, he shook his body thoroughly to get rid of the dust and the scratchy feeling from where the vines had scraped him. But he still felt dirty, and, after all, he was very thirsty as well as hungry. He remembered there was a small stream just over the rise in front of him. He paused, perking up his gray-black ears. Distinctly, he could hear the bubbling of the water.

With a gentle lope, he covered the short distance between the meadow and the stream in very little time. As he ran, several small creatures scampered out of his way. Treek knew they would have made delicious mouthfuls, but he was too anxious to get to the water to be distracted from his course. Upon arrival at the sparkling, clear brook, he did not slow his gait, but continued on until he was wading in water almost up to his neck. Now, he brought himself to a halt and began to slurp the cool, refreshing liquid into his mouth. His long tongue reached out and encircled great droplets of water, drawing them into his awaiting jaws. With meticulous pleasure, he repeated the process over and over again until he felt gorged on the clear liquid.

Once again he pushed himself forward. He swam a few paces in the middle of the stream where the water was over his head. Seconds later he pulled himself out of the water and shook thoroughly a second time. He surveyed his coarse, gray hair and saw that it now glistened because much of the matting had worked itself out of his coat. Satisfied his appearance approximated what it should, he began a slow walk through the forest. As he moved, the liquid inside his belly sloshed about. He could even feel his insides swaying with his movements because of the volume of water he had consumed.

Though he was still quite hungry, he realized instinctively that in his gorged state, he was much too sluggish to pursue game. So he found a comfortable pile of leaves at the base of a nearby tree and lay down for a rest.

As he reclined, thoughts of the delicious smell of rabbit and squirrel delighted his eager taste buds. But there were also thoughts of savory meals enjoyed elsewhere. Gradually, he dispelled the memory of the taste of raw flesh as he brought forth visions of the cultured delights of Laazed. He tried to become disgusted with the dining habits of the dog, but he no longer could. Both types of food seemed appealing to him. He forced himself to remember when he had never partaken of flesh, but he couldn't remember why he did this.

A composite of two faces suddenly came into his mind. Dejung mingled together with the gentle countenance of a she-dog, the she that had given him life and suckled him, then abandoned him along with his brothers and sisters to find their own way in the world. She had been right, of course. He did have to go out on his own eventually. But the other — perhaps he had been right too. Dejung had not really wanted him to leave. Maybe both were right; one did need to know when to go and when to stay, but he was unsure he had ever learned that lesson.

It seemed strange mingling the memories of Dejung with thoughts of the one who had suckled him. But somehow it seemed appropriate also.

Soon the thoughts of distant stars and nearby rabbits all blurred in his mind, and he dozed off.

A loud crashing startled him fully back to consciousness. There — not more than a dozen feet away — were the gaping jaws of a hungry she-tiger. From its stance, Treek realized she was about to pounce, and that he was the intended prey.

Wide-eyed and alert now, he was instantly on his feet retreating as fast as his bony legs would carry him through the jungle. The tiger was right on his tail. They were leaping wildly over fallen trees, through the brush, in and out in a frenzied trail of pursuit and conquest.

Visions of the phantom bear from his nightmares danced in mind as he felt the breathing of the vicious feline close behind him. He knew his legs could not hold out much longer and that the she-beast was much faster than he, even on good days. She was bound to win in open confrontation, also, though he would put up a good fight that she would not soon forget. He knew that tigers seldom attacked dogs or their kinsmen, the wolves, but few dogs would fall asleep in the open so near a stream. Treek cursed himself for such a ridiculous blunder, but a part of him still could not see the obvious.

He felt himself getting weaker and weaker as he ran. There were nicks and stings all over his body from the pricking of his skin by the small bushes as he ran helter-skelter through the brush. But the tiny wounds concerned him little just at this moment when death seemed almost certain and not far off in the making. The tiger would doubtless give a mighty lunge at any moment, and death would have him in her clutches.

From some unknown source he found the strength to push onward, keeping just in front of the jaws of death. The she-beast was practically hovering over him as he made a sharp turn around a clump of briars. Suddenly his destruction was virtually assured for immediately in his path was a massive fallen tree. He had gained a few paces on the tigeress in making his abrupt turn, but now it all seemed for nothing. He knew he could never make an L-shaped or U-shaped turn without the tiger cutting him off from the side, and the tree was much too high for him to bound across.

Just when doom seemed nearest, he spied an opening half covered with branches. He made an awkward plunge toward it, not knowing if the next instance would find him safely through or if his body would be jammed in the small hole and his life devoured.

He hit his head hard as he came down, but half his body had made it through the hole. Branches stabbed him in the side and the tree's rough bark scratched his face, but he squirmed desperately to pull himself through. His struggle beneath the huge tree seemed to take an eternity, but he knew it could not have taken more than a few seconds. Finally, he had pulled free of the tree's embrace and was racing away from the fallen giant.

Breathing more normally now as he ran, he hesitated long enough to glance backward, certain the huge beast could never make it through the hole. What he saw struck terror in his heart again, however, for just at that moment the she-tiger was leaping *over* the fallen tree and charging after him once more. He hesitated no longer but rushed onward at the fastest pace he could muster, certain that he had slowed considerably because of the energy he had had to exert in order to free himself from beneath that tree trunk. Once again, he could feel the tiger's breathing, and he knew the end must be near.

Somehow he found the strength and pushed himself onward, onward, onward.

Momentarily, he noticed that he could now no longer feel the tiger's heavy breathing, and he risked another curious glance backward at his enemy. Strangely, the she was falling behind. He was simply out-pacing her.

Finally, she pulled up and stopped altogether. Treek continued to run a little further, but soon he halted also and looked back at the beast. The other was simply sitting, panting by the side of another fallen tree. Though it was getting dusk, Treek could now see the signs of age on the tiger. That could partially explain why she had been willing to attack him. She was probably so hungry that she thought she could get a good meal by attacking a sleeping dog. No doubt she had been sustaining herself on small animals and had not had a full stomach in weeks or maybe even months.

Treek scolded himself for not realizing the beast was an ancient one immediately.

Now he had little fear of the creature. Even in an open fight, he might have been able to defeat her. But he was weak also. He could use a good meal himself. Raising his nostrils high, he took a deep whiff of early night air. With it, he drew in a variety of smells which his sensors immediately broke down. Most pervading was the smell of the ancient tiger now curled up and breathing heavily not far way. Others were present, though in varying degrees. A skunk had sprayed this area once, but from the density of the smell, that had been a while back. One or two rains had washed the jungle since. Still, the odor was heavy enough to mask everything else, save that of the tiger.

Many other small beasts had passed this way since the skunk. Among them were weasels, chipmunks, squirrels, rabbits, snakes, an opossum, and several variety of birds. But none were recent visitors — not in the last handful of minutes. They had doubtless heard the crashing of the tiger chasing him, and fled. In addition, with the fall of night, many of the creatures would be burrowing into their nests to sleep.

Another distinct smell hung in the air now, however. It was strong, as if the creature were hovering near, but

Treek could not figure what to make of the smell. It was unlike any he had encountered before. It had a sour/bitter/sweet quality to it all at once. And the creature's size was also very much a mystery. It gave off the light odors of a smaller animal while it hung heavy in the air at the same time. It was thoroughly confusing to Treek's nostrils. And though he was very hungry, he decided not to hang around to find out about this unknown quantity. He had had too many surprises lately, and most them had not been to his liking.

He decided to wait till morning to begin his hunt. Quickly he slipped away from the scene of the recent chase. As he glidded quietly through the jungle toward the small cave where he had slept before the mingling, he again caught the odor of man in the distance, and he remembered his old grudge. He decided then that he would not seek out the other, but he knew he would not run from a fight. The time would come when one day he must face the spear-tossing savages again, and then he would make certain the odds were in his favor. He did not intend to lose another battle with those who had caused his imprisonment here!

## CHAPTER FIFTEEN

Treek rode imprisoned in the body of a quadruped carnivore. He looked through the beast's eyes. He smelled nauseating yet stimulating odors through the animal's nostrils. He felt pain and agony with the creature as it fought for its life against other meat-eaters, both its own kind and other species as well. He tasted hot, throbbing tissue and drank blood. He felt; he lived; he fought; he slept — all with the beast. His existence stood in stark contrast to anything he had ever known on Laazed or elsewhere during his short tenure with the Survey Corps. He had been a being of intellect. Now that intellect was subservient to bodily instincts in order for him to survive in this hostile environment and in this alien form.

In the beginning, he returned often to the clearing where he had landed the bio-sampler. Jecke had, after all, become a beloved friend who had come to rescue him, but he was a dedicated surveyor also. Treek had not been surprised that his companion had retrieved the samples he had planted. He longed to know the results of those tests. Would another Laazene vessel bring an exploratory team and maybe later colonists? He wanted to believe that these things would occur, but inwardly he doubted it. Although his people could adapt themselves to its poisonous atmosphere, this world seemed too far off the primary channels to bring others here. Nevertheless, there was always hope that his tests indicated the planet to be a valuable resource for some rare minerals.

He found himself often staring up at the skies, looking for some sign that he had not been completely abandoned. But there was none. Sometimes he tried to reach out with his mind, but nothing came back, and that had been the most difficult for him to accept. Somehow he could accept his exile here, even his imprisonment in alien form — if only he could touch another mind. He had not known how crucial mental contact was until he had lost it. Now he realized that from infancy he had always been in contact with other minds. Others coaxing him, teaching him, scolding him, praising him, helping him, loving him! Now all that was gone. The loneliness that gripped him was devastating. For once, however, he was thankful that his mind was not one but two and that he had his canine memories to stabilize him. Without this other half, Treek was certain he would have lost his sanity. An insane creature would not last long on this world of carnivores, he was certain.

Most of the time he was not really cognizant of the mixture of minds. His actions always seemed natural and logical to him, though to another Laazene or another dog they might seem strange indeed. He was sometimes aware that there must be deviations in his behavior, but he could not be certain what these were. His emotions were his alone, and he was drawn both to the stars and to the meadows and woodlands. They were all his heritage, and that seemed most natural of all.

It was a bright spring day as he stiffed out the scent of a rabbit family that he found his opportunity to settle a long-standing score. He was uncertain exactly how long he had been on this world, but that no longer concerned him. At first, he had counted the days, but he had given that up as a fruitless and frustrating exercise. Only years later would he resume the effort. As winter had closed in, he found it necessary to put all his ingenuity into just finding food and shelter to stay alive. That latter had been necessary when he returned one day to his cave to find a family of his cousins, the wolves, had moved in. Later, he saw this as a disguised blessing, for it caused him to abandon his old hunting grounds (and the bio-sampler landing site, as well) and begin a migration southward in search of more moderate temperatures.

Now, he tramped swiftly but quietly through the forest. The rabbits' trail was getting much fresher. He could tell by the scent that there were still several of the animals together. The smell was all distinctly rabbit, but each rabbit, like each dog, had a distinct odor of its own. Mingled with an overall scent that was clearly rabbit were four different odors that he could distinguish. One of these was much stronger and obviously belonged to an adult. That left at least three small ones, perhaps more, in the pack. He could not be certain there were not more because some of the smells overlapped to such an extent that they were difficult to distinguish.

Suddenly, as their scent led him around a large oak, he came upon the pack. Quickly he leaped back out of view behind the tree just as he saw the mother rabbit's ears prick upward.

She must have heard him coming. He stood silently for a moment, forming a plan. His canine instincts told him to rush forward and scoop up a mouthful of food, but his superior intellect forced him to wait. He glanced around the tree trunk. The mother rabbit had gone back to her nibbling at the grass. Good! He was downwind, and she had not smelled him. He quickly took in the scene. There were five small bunnies scattered about the clearing with their mother. Once again he jerked himself back behind the tree and considered the alternatives. He could go for the mother rabbit, but she was across the clearing and would undoubtedly be swifter of foot than her young. Two of the small ones were quite near the tree where he had hidden. He might be able to leap out and kill both of these at once and then go for a third before they had time to scatter. He might feast indeed!

His mouth had already begun watering as he anticipated the tasty meal. His nerves were coiled and he was ready to spring from his hiding place when he heard a loud crashing in the small clearing where the rabbits were. Instantly he sprang into view, but the small animals were gone, all except the mother rabbit which was lying on the grass bleeding from a wound to her head. Near her lay a bloody stone. Treek did not have to look away from the body to realize what had spoiled his plan and his meal. The culprit was man!

It was a lone hunter, for some reason separated from his pack. He was now crossing the clearing to claim his prize. He carried a stone-tipped spear lightly in one hand, and he walked carelessly toward the body, making no effort to examine the area for other predators.

The hunter's cockiness sent a bolt of fury throughout Treek's system. Not only had the savage stolen his meal, but he had the nerve to claim it without checking for dangers. Well, there was one danger the hunter would not have suspected if he had seen it. Treek would wait no longer to take his revenge on the cause of his abandonment.

Before the hunter could reach the fallen rabbit, Treek was upon him. He lunged from beside the oak tree, and in mere seconds he had bounded into the path of the hunter. Barely discerning Treek's form in time, the hunter put up a feeble defense. His hand went upward to protect his face and throat from the striking terror, and, as his arms rose, the tip of his spear nicked Treek's underside. But the unintentioned blow was enough to break Treek's lunge. He fell short of his mark. The man quickly overcame his surprise and gathered his defenses. Instantly, his spear was gripped firmly in both hands as he leaped toward Treek. The dog's nimble feet easily outdistanced the hunter, but not before he had been nicked again by the crude, stone weapon. This time the wound was on his back. A small amount of blood trickled from the spear's tip as the savage pulled it back for a second charge.

Treek realized immediately that defeating man, even a lone hunter, was not going to be the easy victory he had been awaiting.

Now he found himself on the defensive instead of the offensive. He again and again had to leap from the path of the oncoming weapon, as the hunter pressed his attack relentlessly. Several more times the point of the spear dug into his body, but he was always able to jerk away in time to save himself from a fatal blow. He realized that he was once again fighting for his life — that he could not turn his back on this savage to flee, for surely the spear would find its mark before he could remove himself from its range.

The hunter now began to shout strange and disturbing utterances with each lunge. Treek knew that the other felt he was closing in for the kill and that the shouts were probably a part of some hunter's ritual. The man now appeared to be taunting him, making little effort to finish the job he had begun. Each jab of his spear seemed to be intended only to wound the dog in some non-vital area, so the battle could continue. Treek could not understand what joy the man received from prolonging the fight. If the other had the capacity to kill him, why didn't he do it immediately?

His legs were getting weaker and weaker, and he could see blood stains covering the grass. He realized the blood must be his own. He was feeling very tired. A part of him wanted to lie down on the cool grass and let the spear end his agony, but that was not Treek's nature. Neither of his personalities was inclined to quit something once begun. And neither was inclined to lose.

The stings from his wounds were great; he felt as though he had run many miles. But from somewhere he dug up some extra strength. As the savage was making one of his controlled lunges, Treek found the energy to completely sidestep the weapon. Caught off balance with his appointed target removed, the hunter stumbled forward. The tip of his spear stuck into the soft, grass-covered ground.

Instantly, Treek whirled and pounced upon the spear handle, knocking it from the hunter's hand. Quickly, he turned upon the hunter who had fallen onto one knee to catch himself. Treek found more energy to make one final, mighty lunge of his own, and he had no intention of prolonging the fight as this other had.

His mighty jaws found their mark. He bit into the man's neck and twisted and pulled with all the strength his tortured body could muster. He had no desire to spare this foe. He was savoring the long-awaited kill.

Eventually he stepped away and let the other fall face-forward upon the blood-stained grass. The man lay there gasping for a few moments, drowning in his own blood. When Treek was certain his opponent was quite dead, he turned away, carrying his own bleeding, stinging body over to the fallen rabbit. He took the small creature in his mouth and started to chomp down upon the meal, but something stopped him.

He looked back at the bloody body behind him. Why had he done this? Certainly the man had taken his meal from him, but the spear-tosser had not known.

But man was his enemy! Had these savages not destroyed his other body? He tried to quieten his conscience with that, but it brought up another point: Maybe those beings in that clearing where he had landed were only protecting their property, as he had been "protecting" his property, this rabbit.

He turned slowly toward the man. He pushed his aching body back to the scene of the recent battle and let the rabbit fall from his mouth onto the back of his defeated foe.

Somehow the taste of revenge was not sweet, after all.

## CHAPTER SIXTEEN

The leaves turned later that fall, and, as it became cooler, he moved southward again. He repeated the process the next year and the year after that. Soon he even lost track of exactly how many seasons he'd seen come and go on this planet. Survival required most of his concentration, but even that seemed to be getting more and more difficult.

Treek was now encountering many variety of animals with which he wasn't familiar. Some of these had kinsmen among those he knew. He could tell that by their similarities of scent. But many others were completely new to him.

And there were other surprises. Once he came across a pack of what must have been his distant relatives. They had that hardy and enticing dog smell, but it was mixed with something peculiar and repugnant. Treek had a hard time putting a handle on it, but finally he concluded it was the smell of the dead, of rotting flesh. These creatures also had other differences from his kind. Their bark and growl was totally foreign to him. Oh, he could make out the general tone of anger and fear, but nothing more specific than that. The intelligent portion of his mind had always found the vocabulary of dogs totally insufficient, with grunts and growls having only general meaning — but he could understand these strangers even less than he could the wolf. Quickly he made his departure from them, breathing a sign of relief when he had placed many miles between himself and the eaters of rotten flesh.

The meeting gave him pause to think again on his state in life that night as he lay resting under a low-hanging rock. He licked his lips to savor the last bits of the new delicacy he had just devoured, and he tried to catch his breath. Somehow that chase had tired him more than it should have, and he wondered how he'd ever eluded that tiger or the hunter-man years ago if a simple chase tired him this much. He thought of the pack of rotten flesh eaters and of the packs of wolves and many other dogs he'd encountered. He could see value in those packs, for through the team effort a meal might be captured with much less effort than he had just put forth. But then it would also have to be shared, and he had little desire to split his food up that many ways.

Vaguely he could remember that he had once been part of a pack himself, years ago, but he had become separated from the others and then taken up residence in a small cave. Before he could find his way back to his companions, his other self had landed and been attacked by the humans. That was followed by the uniting of minds and the battle that had damaged him. After recovering from his wounds, he had felt little desire to continue his search for his former companions. Besides, he had reasoned, they were doubtless far away by then. Now he thought fondly of his brothers and sisters of that pack, of Brown Paw, the leader, and Moon Barker and Night Whiner, as well as all the rest. He wondered what had become of them. How many had died on the hunt or been wounded by the sharp tooth of the enemy? He realized that he would long ago have been dead himself were it not for his telekinetic medical abilities. These had preserved him after he'd received many mortal wounds. He thought of his former companions again and felt sorry for them because they didn't have the gift of self-healing. But, as he remembered, there was also another feeling. It was one which had been growing inside him for a long time.

He felt the call to companionship more and more. In the first days of his exile here, he missed the contact of others greatly, but slowly he'd brought that under control. He made it subservient to the need for food and water and shelter. But he knew he couldn't always keep his emotions in check, for he could feel them creeping to the forefront of his thoughts. Several times before he had beaten them off. He fought them back and stood alone. This time he wasn't successful. He was yearning for another.

From his hazy memory, he conjured up fond images of Black Ears. They had run together as puppies, chasing rabbits and squirrels and all manner of small things through the meadows. She had been his favorite. But she had begun to change. She was no longer a pup. She was no longer interested in puppy things. And he'd lost her, lost her forever to the older dogs. Things might have been different eventually if he hadn't...gotten lost...and this hadn't happened. As he thought of her, dead probably these many years, her image melted and was replaced by a mosaic. Black Ears was still there, but so were two others also lost to him. He longed to again be with Guin and Pera, too. There was no separating the image of the two Laazenes and the dog's, but that didn't disturb him. In fact, it was a rather pleasing thought.

Suddenly he was gripped by the realization that a part of that picture might never avail itself to him again. Instantly the joys of his memory turned to bitter loneliness.

*"Oh, Jecke, why did you ever leave me here?"* his anguished mind cried out in the mental vacuum.

He stared up at the stars which were now visible, and he tried to locate Laazed's sun. He realized it wasn't visible here — he had tried to see it many times — but he knew the general direction in which it was located. He stared at that portion of the thickly populated sky and remembered.

He slept fitfully that night. At the first crack of dawn, he crawled from beneath the ledge and worked his way toward a nearby stream he had drunk from the day before. As he approached the water's edge, he spied what appeared to be some form of squirrel, and he wondered why he hadn't sniffed the creature out before he caught sight of it. He felt thirsty, but he couldn't let a tender morsel like this go to waste. It looked like he would dine first, then drink.

Slowly, he inched closer to the small, bushy-tailed, brown beast. It had not sighted him yet and was about to drink. He could see that it had more powerful legs than the squirrels he had been acquainted with and reasoned these must be useful to it for running along the ground. He decided to creep as close as he could before divulging his presence. He was ready to leap at any moment should the creature notice him; however, he wanted to catch it off guard with its head down, drinking.

The beast abruptly jerked its head from the water and gazed in his direction. Then there was no more drinking.

Instantly it was off, running rapidly from the water's edge. Treek had been creeping toward it from behind, so the water cut of its retreat in a straight line away from him. Instead, it zipped away from the water at an angle, leaving him only to cut it off by intersecting its path of departure. Even with its swift legs, its escape seemed unlikely.

Now, however, Treek found himself running hard in an attempt to make the intersection point. Gradually it became apparent that he could not, and he found himself running behind the creature as it dashed away. He continued his pursuit for a short time, but his meal was soon lost from sight.

Disappointed, he turned back toward the stream. He was panting hard. His tongue hung from his gaping jaws and dripped liquid as he struggled to move himself along. He felt thoroughly exhausted.

That chase just should not have been this hard, he told himself. Granted, the ground squirrel was fast, but he had had the advantage of surprise and a planned course of attack. It just should never have gotten away. They had not run that far, but still he could hardly walk. Finally, he was forced to stop and lie down on a clump of coarse grass to rest. After a long time in which he lay there in a near stupor, he pulled himself up and once again turned toward the stream.

The water tasted very good and refreshing, but he still felt winded. He knew he would have to rest more before he could go in search of another meal.

He found a cool spot in a small, abandoned burrow and dozed off.

When he opened his eyes again, it was already dark. He realized he had slept for the entire day. He felt weak and hungry and still exhausted from that brief chase hours ago. He searched the depths of his memory for an explanation, but he could find none. He just felt too tired to concentrate. Gradually, he slipped back into a fitful slumber.

As he slept, there were dreams of his landing and the fight with the man pack. The thoughts were all jumbled with memories of his flight from the tiger, encounters with other dogs and with wolves and bears. He also caught glimpses of other faces from another time. He fought against the agony of the dreams, finally throwing off the slumber that gripped him. He seemed to feel the exhaustion of all these phantom encounters. He ached all over; there seemed no part of him that was not in pain. But mostly he was just exhausted.

Gradually, however, his mind began to clear. He knew now that his subconscious had told him through his dreams what he had not been able to capture before: This body which housed his double intellect was dying!

*He was dying of old age!*

Through the years he had always been able to heal the wounds of battle, but he had overlooked the obvious. Not only was this body subject to the death call from injury, but from age as well.

The cells of his body were deteriorating. They had been deteriorating all these years, and he had done nothing to slow the process. He had defeated many enemies, but he had overlooked the greatest peril, old age. He cursed himself for his inactivity.

From far away, a voice was calling him. From a small spacecraft labeled with the name "Holingar." It told him that the mind could do anything. Mechanically, he acknowledged Jecke's statement, realizing that he had often overlooked his greatest asset. Now he knew it might cost him his life. But, through it all, he understood that his mind was playing tricks on him.

The foreign thoughts came again, as if his former companion were trying to reach out across the gulf of space and tell him something. He could not give up now; he must use his mind in yet another way and try to save himself once more, the thought-voice told him.

But he was tired. First he must sleep.

*"No!"*

Had that thoughtshout really come from outside him? How could it? His mind was trapped here, and there was no other mind to reach his on this planet!

"*No!*" It came again. "*You cannot sleep! You must act if you're going to save that deteriorated body. You must seize control of your mental abilities while you still can. This may be your last chance!*"

It was Jecke calling to him! There was no doubt. But how? Had his former captain so thoroughly mastered the mind that he could reach across the emptiness of space? That could not be done, Treek assured himself. But again Jecke's thoughts shattered his own.

"*Now! Now! Treek, you must listen to me. You cannot wait. Act now!*"

"*Jecke! Where are you?*" Treek pleaded. "*Come and save me. Why did you leave me here? Why don't you come and take me away?*"

Suddenly, his hopes turned to anger. He spat venomous thoughts at his former companion for abandoning him. He hated Jecke for what he had done.

"*Think of me as you will, Treek, but if you do not act now, you have no hope. You may be trapped in a beast's body, but you still live! And while you live, there is always hope.*"

Slowly now, with much effort, Treek turned his attention to his physical condition. Again, as he had done only hours after he arrived on this lonely world, he pulled his essence downward into himself.

Down.

Down. Down.

Deep he went into another trance, fighting once more for his life.

**Part III**

# DESTINY'S CALL

## CHAPTER SEVENTEEN

Hope.

While you live, there is hope, Jecke had said. Or had he? It seemed unlikely now. Most probably his own thoughts had simply taken Jecke's form, Treek reasoned. But Jecke had seemed so real! Treek could never really be certain that Jecke had not reached across space and saved him.

At any rate, he was whole again. Whole, full, and nourished. For a long time, he had possessed that perpetual vigor of youth, a youthfulness he could retain forever if he continually restored his deteriorating cells. Even though it had been many years since he had discovered he was dying from old age and made that critical first restoration, he still thought about the episode and wondered about Jecke. Now and then he looked up at the stars, seeking in vain for a sign of his people's return.

And he continued to hope.

He *would* live and he *would* hope, but there should be more to hope than just waiting and watching. There must be something he could do to change his situation, to heighten his chances of being rescued — to end this agony of waiting.

As he continued his movement southward and somewhat to the west, he had seen nothing of snow in many years. In fact, he had noted very little change in the seasons in a very long while.

The creatures he was encountering now were often markedly different in scent and shape from anything he had seen further north. Some were huge creatures with long necks. Others had great mounds on their backs. One very large, gray beast even had a long, swaying nose. Treek steered wide of such strange beings, finding plenty of small game for food. He also saw many relatives of his own kind, including several variety of dogs, plus foxes, jackals, hyenas, and a few wolves, even though these were getting more sparse the further south he moved. And there were many who were clearly relatives of man, though these often had long arms and tails and were covered in a variety of furs of diverse colors.

More often than not, the creatures he was seeing traveled in packs, as he had done for most of his life before the mind-mingling. It gave him cause once again to ponder his own loneliness. Sometimes he longed to join up with some of the packs of dogs he encountered, but he instinctively knew he would never be accepted. There were none which bore markings similar to his own gray, coarse fur, and even if he did run into another pack with dogs exactly like him, he probably wouldn't be accepted. Dogs just seemed too suspicious of outsiders not raised among their own packs to let him run with them for long. There seemed no other alternative for him but to continue his life as a loner. Then one day he found an opportunity to change all that.

He was hunting some small animal which must have been a relative to the deer. The small herd was grazing near him in an opening in the dense forest. He had long ago dropped his reluctance to pursue the fleet-footed beasts, finding the chase exciting and exhilarating, whether or not he captured what he pursued. He no longer concerned himself with where the next meal was coming from. With winter no longer a concern, he found abundant game and ate well every day. There were still times when his Laazene intellect brought up the old question of eating flesh, and he would feel guilt for a short time. But that would pass, and he always rationalized that he was now a carnivore on a planet of abundant game. He never killed with malice, but only to eat — except for the time when he had slain that lone hunter-man. Occasionally he tried to remember how a meal had tasted on his home world, but that became more and more difficult as the years passed.

Edging his way around the herd of small deer-creatures, he was trying to find the most likely candidate for his next meal. He had just isolated a possibility when he heard the cry of alarm. Screams of fright and pursuit are not unusual in the jungle, but for some reason this one had broken his concentration. He glanced away from the herd and back toward the jungle depths from which the sound had come. There was something haunting and disturbing about that cry. Something nipped at the fringes of his memory, but he couldn't bring it into sharp focus.

"Ay-e-e-e-e!"

There it was again. Treek knew he had heard that sound before. But not here. Far away. Across space and time his mind raced. To a time long ago. To a world near the center of the galaxy. That was where he had heard it — on Laazed!

It was a Laazene cry of alarm!

Suddenly, he was no longer interested in the small deerlike creature he had been stalking. A new excitement occupied his mind.

Had they come back? Had his people come for him at last? He turned and raced through the dense jungle foliage toward the direction of the sound.

"Ay-e-e-e-e!"

There it was again. Now he recognized it as the frightened cry of a young one. But it somehow sounded alien, as well. Could his memory be playing tricks on him again? Had he forgotten exactly how a Laazene child sounded?

The sound came again as he closed in.

As he jumped over a small bush, the cause for alarm was immediately clear. Here crouched the huge, golden-colored beast with the giant fluff of fur around its neck. Before Treek fully realized what he had done, he lunged into the path of the creature.

It turned its gigantic head in his direction and roared a mighty cry, renting all the courage from him. But somehow he managed to make another pass into the path of the beast. As he did, the large cat flung out a forepaw in an attempt to intersect him. The blow missed, thanks to his nimble footwork. He was certain that if the blow had landed, he would have been lying dead upon the jungle floor. Something in him made him make a a third foolhardy lunge, and, as he did, the cat turned its attention fully to him and charged in his direction.

His feet carried him away, fleeing almost certain destruction. Death was surely on his heals this time and at the moment when victory over his situation seemed so close. He realized that he had not actually seen the beast's prey, but he would doubtless be the next victim anyway, so what did it matter?

Nevertheless, he put on a burst of speed unlike any he had displayed in years. He seemed always to be pursuing or pursued. There was just no other way on this jungle world. And this was one race he could not let himself lose. Treek plunged into an intricate set of maneuvers, moving in and out of the brush that cluttered the jungle floor. The roaring, ferocious beast stayed on his tail throughout it all.

He ran unexpectedly from the dense jungle out upon the fringe of a river bottom. His pursuer's swimming ability was an unknown factor, he knew, but his running ability certainly was not. Instantly, Treek threw himself into the stream and swam with all his might toward the other side. With the splashing and the roar of the stream, he could not discern if he had been pursued into the water. When he pulled himself out on the other side, he saw that he had not.

His angry opponent stood on the opposite side of the stream and growled his disapproval for a few moments, then disappeared into the jungle brush again.

Treek ran along beside the bank of the small river for a while, seeking a shallow place to cross it again. He also wanted to get away from the point where he swam it before in case his former pursuer were lying in wait for him on the other side. Finally he found a good place to cross, and he swam back. Then he plunged into the heart of the jungle again, back in the direction from which he had come.

He hoped that the great cat's previous target had not suffered at the claws of some other attacker while he had been leading the cat away. Treek also realized that there was a danger that the cat itself had by now returned to its original prey and devoured it.

When he arrived at the scene of the recent conflict, his hopes for his own rescue were swiftly shattered.

There, on the jungle floor but a few feet from where the great beast had stood when he first saw it, Treek saw a small version of man, a young "spear-tosser." The cries had not come from a Laazene's lips, after all.

Treek stood as if frozen by disappointment, staring at smaller copy of the creatures who had first attacked him on this world. There was little difference in this one and the other he had destroyed in combat except for size and the tone of its skin which was much darker than the others' had been. He thought of tearing this young one to pieces right here, for man had once again been the cause of his grief. But he hesitated. He was uncertain why. For some reason, he did not attack. Instead he just continued to stare at the man pup. The young one's eyes opened wide in terror, but no sound issued from his throat.

The glistening, dark brown skin of this one fascinated Treek. Aside from its smooth texture, it was very similar to what his had been like.

He also thought of the scream he had heard. It had sounded too much like one of his own people for him to harm this youngster.

But if he could not kill the man pup, could he just leave him here for others of the jungle to do the job for him? No, Treek decided, he couldn't do that either. It was obvious that this young one was wounded; otherwise, he would have fled when Treek led the cat away.

A great flooding of emotion swelled within Treek. This pup had had nothing to do with his abandonment on this planet. Why should he be blamed? Indeed, here was one who needed help. For too long, Treek realized he had thought only of his own needs. Here was his opportunity to help another.

He moved closer to the man pup, but the young one released a shrill scream similar to the one Treek had heard before. Quickly, the dog backed away. He had no thought of harming the youngster, but the other could not have known that. He lay down on the soft grass a few paces away and eyed the other. There was still panic in the pup's eyes, but it had begun to diminish. Treek held his position for a long time, studying this young version of man.

There was pain showing on the other's countenance,

but there was also bewilderment. Treek was certain his own action had startled and confused the man pup. He wanted to examine the youngster more closely to discover the extent of his injury, but he knew if he drew nearer, the other would become alarmed and perhaps scream again. And the more he screamed, the more likely he was to be attacked by other predators who might be in the vacinity.

Treek thought he could read intelligence in the man pup's eyes, but he was certain it was far from anything he had known on Laazed. At best, there was only the bud of an intellect growing here, and it might easily be snipped off long before it could mature. At present, man clearly had the intelligence edge on this planet. He already walked upright and used crude weapons, but there was no clear indication he would go further. If he did, it would probably be millions of years before he could approach that which Laazed had.

He continued to study the young one with growing interest. Treek seemed strangely drawn to him. Perhaps all these years of loneliness were reaching him, mellowing him.

Finally, he stood. He had begun to feel the pangs of hunger, and he reasoned the man pup must feel them as well. Quietly, he disappeared into the jungle but returned a short while later with a small, furry creature in his mouth. He strode over to the young one's side and dropped the still warm dead animal. The other made no attempt to scream this time, but his eyes never left Treek.

After the dog had resumed his former position, the youngster glanced away and picked up a sharp rock. He began to scrape the fur away from the dead animal's body. When he had completed this task, he sank his teeth into the soft flesh and began to eat.

After he had finished his meal, the man pup looked

over at Treek once more. His lips turned upward in
what, Treek recalled, would have been called a smile on
Laazed.

# CHAPTER EIGHTEEN

When night began to descend and bring the long shadows into the jungle, the man cub started to tremble, and Treek instinctively moved closer to him. This time there was no sign of fear as he inched nearer and nearer. By the time it was completely dark, Treek found himself by the other's side. At the sound of a distant bird's call, the youngster jerked and Treek nuzzled him. The other reached out and gently stroked his back.

Treek knew that the two of them would be lucky if they got through the night alive. They were too exposed here on the jungle floor. Too many predators prowled the night. They had been lucky that the huge cat had not come back already to claim its prize, but night was probably their most vulnerable time. If it planned to return, it would doubtless do it now.

He thought of fleeing, of saving himself. Even one accustomed to the jungle ways like he was would have difficulty in finding shelter this late, but there was more of a chance if he were alone. He could outrun many who would endanger him. But here, there was little chance. They were just sitting, waiting for danger to come to them. If it came, there would be little choice but to stand and fight.

None of the alternatives seemed desirable. Treek knew that if he left the young one alone, the other had no hope. He questioned the youth's chances even if he remained, giving up his own life. Secretly he called himself a fool for endangering his own existence for this man pup. That he had remained seemed sheer folly, but he was not about to leave now.

He dozed briefly from time to time, but first one sound, then another would bring him to full alert. Once he heard the sound of crashing through the brush, and he knew a life-and-death pursuit was in progress nearby. He restrained himself, keeping in check his desire to issue forth with the dog's sound of alarm. Soon the crashing came to an abrupt end, and so, he knew, had another life. This was the way of the jungle. On another occasion, he saw a pair of glowing eyes staring through the jungle brush. He sniffed deeply but could not distinguish the eyes' owner among all the other smells of the jungle. He kept his own eyes glued to those others, wondering, all the while, if they were staring at his human companion and him. Were they being sized up for a meal? Presently the glowing eyes disappeared from view, and Treek became even more apprehensive. Now that they were no longer visible, Treek had visions of a mighty jungle cat closing in for the kill. But the danger never materialized.

And so it went all night long. First one thing and then another. But miraculously daybreak came, and the two of them were still in the same place undisturbed. Treek could not understand how it had happened. He just accepted it joyfully.

Now that it was light, the youngster began to chatter in a strange, guttural man tongue. He was speaking to Treek. It was clear that he now thought of the dog as his ally. He happily rubbed Treek's back and smiled broadly. He seemed to be taking their safety rather matter-of-factly. Treek recalled primitive cultures he had studied at Deame, reflecting that some blamed their misfortunes on bad gods and good fortunes on good ones. Perhaps that was what this man pup was doing now. Maybe he saw Treek as an instrument of a good god sent to save him from the jungle terrors. Or perhaps he saw Treek as the god himself. That thought intrigued Treek. He thought about it for a little while. Finally, his illusions of grandeur were punctured, however, when he remembered that he could not even free himself of this dog's shell. Some god he was.

The young one rubbed one of his legs, and Treek realized this must be the cause of his predicament. He watched the other closely and nudged the leg to see the other's reaction. Afterwards, he concluded that probably no bones were broken, that it was just a twisted ankle or sprain. If he could only have worked his telekinetic medicine on the other, the young one would be fully restored in a matter of minutes, Treek knew. But he realized that wasn't possible. He was also aware that they could not spend another night here, for they couldn't possibly be so lucky again. Somehow he must persuade this one to attempt to walk. If he did, maybe they could get him back to his people or at least to safer ground.

Now the man pup was rubbing his stomach, and Treek knew that hunger had attracted his attention. As a matter of fact, he felt hungry himself. The matter of moving to safer ground could be shelved for a while, but he would think on a solution. Perhaps it would come to him while he hunted.

He didn't like leaving the youngster alone, but he rationalized that this was the only way for them to get food. So, off he went again in search of a meal. This jungle was a rich source of small game, and he had not gone far before he came across, quite abruptly, a tasty morsel resting very still. At once, his target was off and away, but Treek caught him quickly in one mighty leap.

After the catch, he placed his prey upon the soft jungle grass and examined it. Though it had some similarities to rabbits, he knew this wasn't one. Its longer ears and legs distinguished it, but most of all, there was practically no scent. He searched his memory and recalled that this was a larger relative of the rabbit called a hare. Because of their lack of strong odor, he had tasted few of these, and not in years. If he had not happened on this one almost accidentally, he would not have it. Also, if he hadn't startled it, the creature's strong legs might have taken it far from his jaws of death. He had the urge to tear into the juicy flesh and gorge himself, but he remembered the man pup. He realized the hare was enough of a meal for both of them.

Back at the spot where he had left the young one, Treek quickly tore the hare in two and gave half to his companion. Without ceremony, he then gulped down his half and again disappeared into the jungle.

While on his way back to the youngster with the hare, an idea had occurred to him, and now he was anxious to attempt it. Swiftly he searched the jungle floor. He felt handicapped because he could not use his nose for what he sought. He remembered too that he had lost a better set of eyes to a group of men on the soil of this world years before. He could have used those eyes now in attempting to save one of their kind. But he felt no real bitterness, only remorse.

Finally he came upon something which he felt might fill his need.

With mighty jaws, he reached down and took the broken limb and began to drag it along the jungle floor back to the man pup. When he arrived exhausted some time later, he laid the limb at the side of the other.

The man pup looked at him quizzically.

Treek stared back into those other eyes, eyes which showed a spark of potential. Surely this youngster could understand what he had intended. Anxiously Treek waited for the other to pick up the limb, but he made no effort to do so.

The canine glanced upward. The sun was well past mid point in the sky. His hunting and searching and dragging had taken much time. They could not wait much longer.

He wanted to cry out to his companion with his mind to tell him of his plan. But he knew the effort would be fruitless. Or would it?

Had the dog's mental energy simply been drained before, due to his injuries? Perhaps he *could* speak to the youngster with his thoughts. At least he could try.

He closed his eyes and concentrated deeply, attempting to make his idea known to his companion.

Slowly he opened his eyes and stared at the other. Still the youth sat unmoving.

Once again, Treek closed out the rest of the world and concentrated. He wiped out all thought of everything else, concentrating entirely on one solitary bit of information. Over and over again he repeated the thought.

Finally, he opened his eyes once more. When he did so, he found the youth studying the limb he had placed nearby. Gradually, the youngster's hand went out and picked up the object. He examined it slowly and methodically, turning it over and over, looking at all sides.

Suddenly he was a flash of motion. He grasped the rock he had used for skinning the animals Treek had given him. He began to use it quickly to slash away at the stubs of leaves and brush on the limb. He grasped it by one end and began to pull against it.

Using the limb for support, he began gradually to rise. He had taken most of his weight off the injured foot. Up he pulled himself until finally he was in a full standing position. He looked over at Treek and laughed, then uttered more phrases in his strange, guttural tongue. Treek was certain these must be words of joy and praise.

Slowly, the youngster began to move about. He *could* walk again, thanks to the crutch Treek had given him!

Treek was caught up in this moment of joy too, for he had caused it.

But secretly he questioned how much he had really done.

## CHAPTER NINETEEN

His name was "Jamak." His father and others of his pack had already given up looking for him when he and Treek appeared. Treek also learned that his kind, the male man pups, were called "boys." Females were "girls." These became "men" and "women" when they reached a certain age and did certain deeds.

But Treek did not learn all this immediately. When he'd turned away to leave once Jamak was deposited safely, the young one restrained him. He hugged Treek and wept. So, Treek decided to stay for a short time with the boy and the man pack, which he learned later was called a "tribe." As a result of his varied experiences of man, he was anxious to observe their kind more closely, and this seemed a good opportunity. His presence in the tribe's cave, after a few days, seemed to be accepted rather matter-of-factly by most members of the group.

In less time than it took for the moon to make one complete orbit of this planet, he learned to understand all the tribe's words. But he could not speak them. He tried many times, though when Jamak or other tribal members heard, they would scold him or throw small stones at him to stop his "howling."

One evening, he lay near the campfire (something which his canine instinct had had difficulty in accepting as an instrument of good as well as ill) and listened. Combuc, the tribe's "healer of the sick and speaker to the spirits" — the leader of Jamak's people — was telling of the dangers of the tree spirits. Treek wished he could debunk such nonsense and help these primitives overcome their fear of nature, but there seemed little hope for that.

"When the great Leaf Spirit comes, the wind blows through the trees, and the animals run. They know not to oppose the Mighty One. Why aren't we as smart?" Combuc asked. He had been talking for several minutes, "informing" the other men why that day's hunt had failed to produce adequate game. Treek smiled inside and asked why Combuc hadn't forecast the failure. It always seemed easier to find causes when one was looking backward instead of forward.

Surely all these people weren't that stupid. But he had seen nothing to convince him otherwise. He thought back on all the legends and mythology of Laazed. His people had also believed in spirits and demons and all manner of supernatural creatures, and they had overcome it. However, he recalled, it had taken them millions of years. Now, here he was, a product of that superior culture, inhabiting the body of a lowly beast (half his mind bristled at that thought, but he continued his contemplations). And he wasn't certain that he was not viewed as a god or a spirit by at least some of the People of the River's Bend, as they called themselves. His saving of Jamak must indicate that this dog's body was possessed by the spirit of some ancestor. Treek chuckled again. This body was indeed "possessed," but they could not have understood it if he had told them.

The campfire ceremony was breaking up, and the people were moving away from the mouth of the cave. Each was going to his respective "home" in the mammoth abyss. Treek, too, climbed to his feet. He stared out at the jungle beyond. All was blackness, but he could hear the sound of the rushing water from several yards below. He had almost become so used to it that he no longer heard the gurgling and sloshing.

"Miskah," Jamak called. "Come here."

Treek looked around and realized his young "master" was calling him. He had finally gotten use to his new name also.

Jamak slapped his knee and smiled his friendly smile. Treek strolled over to his side.

The boy reached out and patted him gently on the neck.

"One day I will join the hunt, too. When I'm tall enough to reach the Mark of Man." He glanced over at a groove scratched in the cave wall about six feet from the floor. Treek had already become familiar with the rite of passage practiced by the People of the River's Bend. He knew that a boy became a man when he could reach the mark with his right hand while standing flat-footed upon the floor. The boys of the tribe were often testing their height and stretching ability at the mark.

"When I become a hunter, there'll be great amounts of food for everyone. Jamak the mighty will destroy our enemies. We'll have no more hunts that fail."

Treek heard a low grunt near him, and he glanced around to see Combuc staring at Jamak.
The boy saw it too, for he added: " — except when there are Leaf Spirits around!"

Treek was certain the youngster did not place as much credence in Combuc's stories as some did, but he knew that his master's will must bow to that of the tribal leader. If not, Jamak could be expelled from the tribe, if he were lucky, or stoned to death, if he were not. It was apparent that the chief had resented Jamak's presence since the lad had emerged from the jungle following his ordeal. It seemed Combuc had foretold the boy's death in the jaws of a mighty black panther, and Jamak's return had proven the other wrong. Treek suspected that Combuc's own fear of "Miskah" was the only thing that had saved the boy from harm.

Jamak continued to pat "Miskah" lightly as they moved toward his family's cove. Treek could not completely keep his canine instincts in check. As they moved away from the tribal chief, a low growl pushed itself from his throat.

"No, Miskah. Don't! Combuc could kill you with his swift spear." The boy bent low and continued talking in a quieter voice. "But don't worry, someone will get him some day for his evil ways." That was an echo of a comment Jamak had heard Rul, his father, make to his mother, Baaka. Treek knew this, but Jamak's restatement of it stirred his optimism.

He had gathered that no one in the tribe cared a lot for the leader. He had overhead several conversations and grumblings which were enough to tell him that. But none would oppose Combuc openly. They all feared his strength and his skill with weapons. If that wasn't enough, he talked with the spirits, and the People of the River's Bend weren't about to turn the spirits against them. Treek realized these people should be led out of the darkness of superstition into the light, but even if he could talk to them and tell them, they would just see him as a spirit also. It wasn't really his concern, anyway, he concluded. Let the rabble wallow in their stupidity.

He curled up at his spot on the cave's dirt floor, and Jamak moved on to his place and pulled a moldy deerskin over his young body. His father, mother, and three sisters were nearby.

At first, Treek had found this cave too musty and filled with the vile odor of men to sleep well. He wondered how these people could go unbathed as they did. His own skin crawled if he didn't take a dip in the river from time to time. Besides, the water was cool and refreshing. The cave's damp earthen floor was not really to his liking either. But he had overcome these concerns eventually and learned to sleep near Jamak.

This night, as he settled down, he watched the fire at the cave's mouth flicker lower and lower and everything around him get darker and darker. Just before the flame had completely extinguished itself, Cranic got up and stirred it and placed more wood on it. In the renewed light of the campfire, he studied the wall markings near him. They had obviously been the product of man, but he judged their esthetic value very low. Most of the marks were simply that to Treek — only "marks."

He couldn't discern what, if anything, they were supposed to represent. Others were recognizable as very crude outlines of animals, including man. All the marks appeared to have been scratched on the cave wall with charcoal, probably with half-burned sticks from the campfire. Treek wondered if the markings were made by the People of the River's Bend or by other humans who had occupied this cave previously. He had never seen anyone marking on the cave, but he had been with these people only a short time, so he did not consider his evaluation as final.

He was about to doze off when he heard the distant cry of his cousin, the hyena. He raised his head and stiffed the air, but all he caught was a snoot full of smoke from the recently stirred campfire. He sneezed and rubbed his nose, trying to get the irritating odor out of his nostrils, then he sneezed again.

There was a rumbling in the direction of Baaka and Rul. He recognized Baaka's voice. She was apparently speaking to Jamak's father. Presently Rul spoke.

"Quiet, dog!" he shouted, and Treek knew the wrath

was directed at him, since he was the only dog in the cave.

There was more rumbling, as others of the tribe chimed in, some scolding Treek for his noise and others admonishing Rul to "be quiet" himself.

Presently all was still again. Treek's nostrils continued to burn with the tingling irritant of smoke, but it was not as bad as before. He kept his head low and still. Finally, after what seemed like hours and may have been that long, he slipped into a fitful slumber.

As he slept, the old dreams came back. The bear was chasing him into the giant tree trunk; men were beating his shattered form; he was listening to Zokken's tales of space and stars. They were mixed, varied and quite unnerving. He awoke with a start, but the dreams seemed to continue. Treek thought once more of his long lost home on Laazed, of Pera and Guin and of his lost hopes for a life of glory among the stars. Sometimes he questioned his own sanity and wondered if all his memories of his home across the stars were just dreams — tormenting nightmares — of a deluded mind. But he could not accept that either. Occasionally, he wished he could, but he was too much of a realist for that. He knew what he had been. It was too much a part of him to abandon now. But it was gone, gone forever. He wished his memory would let him have peace. His people would never return for him. He was lost. Why couldn't he just accept what he was and live life as a dog?

His thought-chain was suddenly broken by the sound of Jamak's snoring. How long had he been with the boy? A few weeks. It seemed like more. He became conscious of a bitter taste in his mouth, but he couldn't spit it out. He realized finally that it was coming from within. He had had great talents, and he had squandered them, especially those of the mind. But perhaps he still had some! He had wasted many, but there was still something left, still a spark. He had used it once to save Jamak. Why hadn't he tried to reach the boy's mind again? Was he afraid of failure? Or success maybe? In the dim haze of the campfire light, he could barely see the markings on the cave wall. However, they were still undecipherable, as though they were undeveloped. Though he had lived countless years on this planet in his present form, he realized he was like the cave markings. He still was an unknown quantity — undeveloped.

And he remembered Jecke and those phantom thoughts which had appeared to reach out to him across space. He knew they must have been a delusion, but the thoughts — whether from his own or another mind — had been real. They were what saved him. They had kept him alive. He still possessed that hope, that ardent desire to be rescued and taken again to his own, but that did not prevent him from finding himself here. Zokken had found himself and become more content with his life — shortened though it was — than any other Laazene he had ever known. Perhaps it had been Zokken's zest for living which he had been seeking all along though he had not let himself slow down enough to find it. His search for a way to return home would continue, he resolved. But, like Zokken, he must find himself and become what he could become.

The dirty, smelly, small boy near him gave out with a great snort, and Treek turned to look upon his sleeping form. Somehow he felt no longer offended as he had when he first set eyes on Jamak's countenance.

Eventually, he shifted his gaze back toward the mouth of the cave, and he noticed a glimmer of the first light of dawn.

## CHAPTER TWENTY

As the years passed, the changes in Jamak were striking. His muscles had begun to grow perceptibly and hair appeared on his dark brown chest and elsewhere where previously there had been none. His voice seemed gruffer and he had grown taller by several inches. It was no surprise to his companion "Miskah" that he was soon able to reach "the Mark of Man."

Jamak was no longer a boy. And his initiation into manhood, as it was with all males of the tribe, was to join the hunt. Like all the boys of the People of the River's Bend, Jamak had been practicing spear-throwing so he would be ready for the great day when it finally came. Treek had had much confidence in his young "master," but now that the day of maturation was at hand, he began to have his doubts. Treek studied Jamak as he stood with the other members of the hunting party, and he knew the young man still had much growing to do. He did not have the muscles of Combuc or the fleetness of foot of Cranic or the ability in spear-throwing of Boondar. And Treek was certain Jamak lacked the wisdom of Rul, his father.

As it was a day of joy for Jamak, it was a time of mixed emotions for Treek. Certainly, "Miskah" had been a faithful companion to Jamak during those growing years. He had romped with the boy and shared his workload when possible. But throughout it all, Treek had felt great disappointment, for he had not been able to duplicate his success in thought-projection again. Sometimes he even questioned the success of his first effort. Perhaps it had been coincidence alone. Perhaps Jamak had simply figured out what could be done with that limb all by himself and had not read Treek's thoughts at all. Maybe Treek hadn't tried hard enough to get through to Jamak. Was something inside still making him hold back? He had not given up attempting to reach Jamak, but, after all these years, his efforts were less frequent.

He watched as the hunting party set out at the break of day on the morning following Jamak's accomplishment. Combuc had never allowed Treek to accompany the hunters, despite Rul's repeated statement that "the dog could do much of the work for us in finding game." Combuc had maintained that Treek's presence would upset the spirits of their ancestors and spoil the hunt. But Treek had once overheard Rul complaining to Baaka that "Combuc is a fool. The dog's nose would make our hunt much easier." Jamak's mother had quietened her husband quickly, fearing for his safety, less he unleash the wrath of the tribe's leader.

As the hunting party disappeared from sight, Treek knew he could not let Jamak go on his first hunt without him. He slipped quietly from the cave and flowed in the direction of the hunters. Jamak had been under Combuc's order to watch Treek until the hunters had been gone for a long time, but with Jamak now a member of the hunting party, there was no one to keep an eye on him. It was one of Combuc's little oversights, so he would take full advantage of it. Oh, he planned to keep well out of sight, for Treek knew, even though Jamak was now a hunter, he would be in trouble if Combuc spotted his dog. The fact that he had not assigned anyone else to watch Treek would not deter Combuc. Logic never worked on his kind.

The trail was easy to follow. Men always left not only their strong and oftentimes offensive smell but plenty of other signs that they had passed a certain way. There were footprints in loose soil, broken and bent twigs, holes in the ground from their spear points and all manner of other things. Treek needed none of these latter, for the scent was ample for him to follow. He supposed he could have followed the party's scent for up to three days after they had passed. But he was conscious of these other signs of man and was confident that he could have followed the hunters even without a scent to guide him.

The warm sun beat down upon him, and even though he was insulated from its direct rays by his hair, he felt warm and uncomfortable. He disdained Combuc's choice of trails, as he did most of the tribal leader's ways. Had he been in charge, he would have taken a much cooler path, and he would have found more game. Few tender morsels were likely to fling themselves in front of the hunter's spear in this heat. Besides, it was too open. The floor of the covered jungle would have been much more to his liking. There would have been plenty of game, and the canopy of foliage would have shielded the hunters from the direct rays of the sun. But Treek suspected that more than stupidity kept Combuc from the heart of the jungle. The man was driven by fear, the fear of ignorance and superstition. He feared not only the beasts that inhabited the jungle but the "spirits" that inhabited the beasts, as well.

Treek had been closing on the hunters for some time, and, though they were still out of sight, he could hear them. They made no effort to remain quiet, and this too disturbed him. He wondered how these beings had survived as long as they had without the rudiments of hunting knowledge, one of the foremost of which was to remain absolutely silent while stalking a prey.

He could hear the loud and boisterous voice of the chief laughing and barking out commands to the other hunters. It made Treek's skin crawl and hair stand on end. The man was truly an imcompetent, but not one of these mighty hunters had the courage to stand against him. Any two of them could have banded together and defeated Combuc, even if he were the most powerful — but that had never occurred to their feeble minds! Occasionally he asked himself why he had stayed with the likes of them, but he always remembered Jamak. He felt the "young man" — for he was no longer a boy — had promise, promise to amount to more than the likes of Combuc. That's why he remained. That was not all, he knew. But the rest he would not let himself admit.

Suddenly, shouting brought full focus on the hunting party. He did not have to hear the words to make him understand the cause for alarm. His nose warned him first with a frighteningly familiar odor.

"Tiger! Tiger! Run for the trees!"

Treek recognized Zumbac's voice and immediately leaped into action. Although his impulse was to turn and flec the savage beast, his superior intellect mastered his canine instincts and forced him in the direction of the outcry.

Topping a small rise, he could see the hunters of the People of the River's Bend scattering in all directions, all except one. One man had stumbled and the tiger was making straight for him. Treek strained his dog's eyes to make out the identity of the fallen one.

Rul! It was Rul, Jamak's father, and he was a certain target of death if something didn't happen to distract that tiger immediately.

Treek thought of throwing himself at the creature, but that would have proven a worthless sacrifice. The beast must weigh more than five hundred pounds and would make quick work of him, then move on to Rul before the other could pull himself up.

Thoughts were rushing through his double mind at the speed of light, and he was discarding idea after idea while he watched the beast closing in for the kill. In desperation, his mind cried out.

*"Jamak! Turn back! Turn back! Turn back! Turn back!"* Immediately he saw his young "master" halt and glance back at the thundering machinery of death.

"No, Evil One! Get away!" Jamak shouted, reversing his course and running wildly toward the tiger. He flung his arms out and continued to scream as he ran, making an uncanny sight, even for one used to the ways of man. For the tiger, who weighed several times as much as his young attacker, it must, nevertheless, have been a disturbing sight. Abruptly, the beast stopped short of its mark and stared in awe toward Jamak. Meanwhile, Rul had pulled himself to his feet and was limping toward the nearest tree.

"No, Jamak, get away!" he shouted over his shoulder as he hobbled away.

Immediately the tiger shifted its gaze back to its original target and would have doubtless resumed its flight toward Rul had Jamak obeyed his father's warning. But the younger man did not, so the tiger was torn between two targets, apparently overawed at the audacity of this puny one attacking him.

But only for a split second did it waver, however, before turning its attention full toward Jamak. By now the young man was less than a dozen yards away, and, as the beast made its first lunge toward Jamak, it was met full force by the impact of the young hunter's stone spear in its throat. There was another shout from Rul's direction, and, seconds later, half a dozen more spears sprayed from the surrounding trees and punctured the tiger's body.

A mighty roar from the gigantic cat split the air, and it halted its lunge once more. Furiously it lashed out at one of the spears protruding from its body, succeeding only in pushing it deeper into its flesh. There was another fierce cry, this one of pain, and the great beast fell dead.

Treek had remained out of sight during the course of the battle, but now he could hardly restrain himself. He wanted desperately to join Jamak in this moment of victory. After all, the triumph was his as well as Jamak's. A warm glow began to spread over his body, and he knew it wasn't simply from the heat of the sun.

With much effort, he held his impulses in check. He did not want to risk destroying Jamak's glory and bringing on the wrath of Combuc, so he remained out of sight and watched what transpired among the members of the hunting party.

Jamak and Rul's companions were slow to alight from the safety of the trees even after their own weapons had slain the mighty tiger. Finally, one by one, they began to jump to the ground and walk over to the fallen beast. Already, Jamak had been joined by his father, and they were looking over the carcass. One of the last to arrive on the scene was Combuc.

"The cat spirit is beaten. The day is ours," he mumbled, apparently speaking to no one in particular but for all to hear.

"My son will have a great trophy from his first hunt," Rul said, addressing the chief. "No one would dare deny the courage of a hunter who has attacked a tiger."

"Or his stupidity," Combuc put in. "Attacking a tiger is really a stupid thing to do. No hunter in his right mind — no seasoned hunter — would charge a beast like this one." He indicated the tiger with the point of his spear which had been one of the few not flung at the terrible and powerful menace, now vanquished.

Combuc paused and look around at the faces of the other hunters of the People of the River's Bend, then he resumed his statement.

"I do not recognize this skin as belonging to Jamak. He did not kill the cat spirit alone. Many of us share in the glory of this victory. So, not only must the meat be shared by all, but also the skin."

Even from a distance, Treek could make out the displeasure in his young master's face, but Jamak made no move to counter the chief's order. And neither did Rul or any other member of the hunting party.

Again Treek had to remind himself to stay out of sight. He could see the wisdom in sharing the tiger's meat. It should be for the whole tribe. But how could its skin be shared by all? Instantly he recognized this as another of Combuc's acts of villainy. The "sharing with the tribe" meant the tiger's skin would become the property of the tribal leader, since he was the symbol of the tribe. Treek wanted to make a mighty lunge himself — this one toward the master villain. He would tear Combuc's throat out, even as he had that other man's years ago. But he again restrained himself. No, he had been wrong before. He knew he could never again kill just to vent his emotions.

But he also knew something must be done to rid these people of their ignoble leader.

## CHAPTER TWENTY-ONE

It had become increasingly difficult for Treek to note the passage of time. Now that he lived in a climate where there were few seasonal changes, this planet's years slipped by almost imperceptibly. But Treek had found one way to tell that the years wcre marching onward: the children. Those who were young ones when he'd joined the tribe were now either hunters or bearers of young themselves. Jamak had been only a boy when Treek had saved him from death in the jungle. Treek had seen him change from that to the young hunter who saved his own father from the tiger. And from that to the man who now towered over most of the other People of the River's Bend. There was also the young girl, Mawac, whom the hunters had found wandering near their cave. Under protest, she had accompanied them back to their home. Not a few of these killers of mighty beasts were bitten and clawed by the girl who spoke a strange tongue and refused to eat for many days. Finally, however, she had given up her struggle against the inevitable and adapted to the ways of the People. Recently, Jamak had taken her to wife, and now they had a new young one of their own. Seeing Jamak and Mawac together and the love they shared brought back memories for Treek of a time and place far removed.

Treek had known that he wasn't mentally mute for a

long time. Jamak's responses to his thought impulses over the years had proven that. He was never certain when he could get through to his "master," however, though he had been able to draw some definite conclusions about his own present mental abilities. The first was that they were quite limited. The mental energy produced by the dog's brain which housed his mind was very weak. In fact, it was so weak, Treek was surprised that any mental transmission was possible at all. He was certain that he was incapable of carrying on any normal mental conversation, but he was just as certain that some reception of his thoughts had taken place. During the past several years, he had tried many times to project his thoughts to others among the People of the River's Bend. Only Jamak had seemed responsive at all and that only on a very limited basis. After countless experiments, Treek was sure that Jamak could receive him, but just during certain periods and under certain qualifying circumstances. Only during periods of great stress or emotion could Jamak receive ideas from Treek's thought-projections. Not pure conversation; Treek had decided that such was impossible with his companion's limited mental receptiveness. Not even simple phrases. He could only pick up the germs of ideas, and these he couldn't even differentiate from his own. He evidently had no inkling that these ideas originated out of his own head. Jamak simply had no idea that Treek was communicating with him.

At first, it had been frustrating. When he'd become convinced that Jamak was receiving his thought impulses after that tiger attack many years ago, Treek had been elated. He felt freed at last from the bondage of his dog's body. He felt that he would once again be able to converse with another, even if that other were an ignorant cave man. Then when he had realized the limited extent of his ability, he withdrew unto himself once more and even left his home with the tribe for a time. But eventually he returned, having come to accept his isolation. He had learned to live with the situation again. He knew when to attempt communications with Jamak, but he also knew that many of his thought impulses fell on infertile ground and were discarded by Jamak before they had an opportunity to grow. Occasionally, however, old ideas came to the surface long after Treek had planted them, and he would be surprised to find Jamak acting on one of his earlier suggestions. Such was the case on this day as he lay quietly in his spot watching the hunting party ready itself for the search for meat. He had been studying the wall markings for the hundredth time and almost dozing when he heard a familiar voice call to him.

"Come, Miskah." It was, of course, Jamak. "In celebration of my new little one, today you will join the hunt."

Treek lay unmoving. He knew the People's custom of allowing new fathers to lead the hunt. But he was certain Combuc would never consent to his coming along. And he was right. Soon he heard the tribal leader's objections.

"No! You know it's forbidden."

"I know *you've* forbidden it," Jamak replied.

"*And* the spirits. I am only the voice of the spirits. They have forbidden this animal to join the hunt. Why do you try to anger them?"

"I'm not trying to anger the spirits. I'm only taking my privilege as leader of the hunt for today. It is my right!"

The discussion was getting louder and had attracted the attention of many — women and children as well as the other hunters.

"You are angering them!"

"I'm only claiming my right. I'm sure Miskah will make the hunt more profitable. If it isn't so, I'll never take him along again. We can use his nose. It'll be useful for sniffing out game even before we can see it — or it sees us!"

"No! The dog cannot come! I forbid it!"

For a moment, Combuc's declaration appeared to put an end to the discussion. Jamak fell silent. The other hunters turned to gathering up their spears and mumbling to themselves. Then abruptly Jamak spoke again, this time louder than before — clearly for all to hear.

"No! You speak for the spirits, perhaps. But you do not speak for all the spirits, Combuc!"

Instantly, all the murmuring stopped and all eyes focused on Jamak, who paused long enough to gaze into his mother's eyes. She gasped and started to weep. Mawac put her little one, Creja,
down among some bear skins and comforted her mate's mother. Treek slowly stood up. Now Jamak continued.

"No, there is one spirit that only I can speak for. That is the spirit of Rul, my father. I speak for my father's spirit, and he wishes Miskah to join the hunt!"

Again, Jamak stared around the cave room.

"Is there any here who would deny this?" he asked. He turned to another of the hunters. "Zil, you heard my father say it — that the hunt would be better off if we took Miskah along. And you, Deebic! And Cranic! You must have heard him also. You know it's the wish of his spirit that the dog accompany us."

He turned back to Combuc, whose face had taken on a swollen, sullen glow. His lower teeth bit into his upper lip, giving his shaggy appearance an even more ghastly look. But the other did not speak to counter Jamak.

There was a long silence.

"Very well," Combuc said, at last, "but I'll not go along on this hunt. I will not hunt with that beast!"

He glared angrily at Treek, who now trotted to the

side of Jamak.

Inside, Treek was laughing. He had won. Jamak had won. Combuc had not dared stand up to the prospect of angering the spirits. How long had it been since he had first urged Jamak to take him along on a hunt? He couldn't remember exactly, but he was certain his "master" had chosen the right moment to make his point. Now he must not disappoint this man.

As he marched from the cave with Jamak and the other hunters, his mind leaped far beyond this primitive hunt. He was savoring the fact that his mind could change things again.

## CHAPTER TWENTY-TWO

It was a hunt. And what a hunt!

The alliance between dog and man proved stunning beyond Treek's wildest hopes. He sniffed out a deer, and Jamak brought it down with one mighty thrust of his spear. Jamak left Burac to guard the kill, and the hunt moved on. With Treek's nose and the spears of the men, they brought down more in a single day than they sometimes had in a week. The laden hunters brought back three zebras, twelve rabbits, eight monkeys, two deer, and a boar.

But they were not welcomed.

Treek had sniffed out his evil odor long before they arrived, but, of course, he had been unable to warn Jamak and the others. So they were surprised to find Combuc holding his spear barring the entrance to the cave.

Jamak laughed when he saw the expression on the other's face and tried to push his way inside with the deer he carried across his broad shoulders. But the tribal leader blocked his path.

"Stand aside, Combuc. Has jealousy loosened your mind?"

"No!" the chief shouted with all the force of his lungs. "You cannot bring that contaminated food inside. I *forbid* it!"

Jamak laughed again. "As I recall, you *forbade* me to

take old Miskah along on this hunt, as well."

"Yes. I tried to warn you — you fool!" Combuc puckered his face into an ugly grimace. "Now you have brought the wrath of the tree spirits down on us." He waved at the other approaching hunters. "All of you, halt! Lay down that meat where you are. You must not bring it inside our home."

"What are you talking about?" Jamak demanded.

"You *are* a fool, Jamak. I warned you not to take that beast along on the hunt." He glared again at Treek, who stood by Jamak's side. Treek glared back and let a slow, steady growl ooze from his throat. "All this meat is contaminated. The spirits are angry, and the only way we can rid ourselves of their anger is to destroy this meat — *and* to chase away this evil thing from our midst."

Combuc glanced down at the dog once more.

Jamak broke into a full, hardy laugh. "You are mad! Your jealousy had driven you completely mad. There is nothing wrong with this meat — nothing that a feast won't take care of. We could eat from it for days, as long as it stays fresh."

Treek's "master" moved again as if to enter the cave. Combuc lowered his spear so that the point was aimed directly at Jamak's midsection. Gradually, Jamak's smile disappeared. Behind Combuc, a woman screamed. Treek recognized the voice as Baaka's.

Slowly, Jamak let the deer slide from his back. His eyes burned deeply with rage. Treek knew this was the moment to touch his companion's mind with a plan to destroy the chief's credibility once and for all. In a flash he had thrown his thought outward and waited to see if his "master" would take up the challenge. He did not have long to wait.

"So you say that the spirits have poisoned this meat?" Jamak asked, anger causing him to slur his words as he stared into the chief's bloodshot eyes.

"That's right. It must be destroyed!"

"I tell you there is nothing wrong with this meat."

Jamak looked around at the other members of his party. They too had laid down their burdens of flesh. None of them spoke in Jamak's defense.

"It's good meat, I tell you," Jamak continued, "and I'll prove it to yau."

"And how will you do that?" Now it was Combuc who seemed on the verge of laughing.

There was a pause as Jamak looked around for support once again. Most of the hunters looked away to avoid his gaze. In his mind, Treek condemned them all for their cowardice. But he also wondered if Jamak had the strength to carry through his plan. He was now convinced that the other had received his thought; he only questioned Jamak's courage to carry it through to completion.

Just as Combuc was about to burst into open laughter, Jamak spoke again. "Yes, I'll prove it. I'll eat this meat myself. That'll prove it's safe far all because, if it doesn't kill me, it won't harm anyone. I will feast tonight while the rest of you go hungry — unless there is someone who will join me."

Again Jamak examined the faces of his fellow hunters. No one spoke.

"Then it's settled. I will eat alone!" he added. "And if I do not die, Miskah will remain and join us on every hunt. If the spirits take me, you can do as you will with this meat and with my family as well."

Treek's ears perked up. He had not thought that. Not the part about Jamak's family. But it pleased him, for Jamak was now acting on his own courage and imagination. All he had needed was a little guidance. Treek felt little concern for Mawac and Creja's safety, for he was certain that there was nothing in the meat which would harm Jamak.

Shortly, all the hunters sat silently around the cave fire. Cranic, as keeper of the flame, stirred it and placed more wood on the blaze. Jamak was chewing the raw flesh of a deer.

The women stood well back from the fire, and now it was Baaka who hugged Mawac and stoked Creja's tiny, peaceful face. Treek studied the small one, realizing how oblivious she was to the tensions around her. She slept.

He too stayed back from the hunter's circle. He watched as Jamak ate from a rabbit and zebra as his comrades sat around him, no one uttering a sound. Combuc's sullen face showed his hatred and anger toward Jamak. He sat opposite his challenger, across the campfire.

Darkness was setting in. Treek could hear the nocturnal sounds of the jungle outside the cave.

Suddenly Combuc jumped to his feet in a frenzy and began to shout again. "You fool! You kill yourself with that poison meat. Only I can save you now. I can ask the spirits to release you from their curse if you will only drive that thing" — he glared again at Treek and grimaced — "out of our home. If you do not, you surely will die!"

"No, I won't," Jamak replied slowly. "I've already said it. Miskah remains! He saved my life when I was only a boy. He's my dearest friend. I wouldn't betray him now that he's growing old. Besides, he's possessed of a good spirit and will join me on many hunts. He is the spirit of good. All the spirits you speak of are evil!"

"You're the biggest fool ever to hunt with the People! But, no matter, I'll speak to the spirits; I will say my chants and save you anyway," the chief replied after a long silence.

What was this? Treek was momentarily perplexed. Then he realized it was another of Combuc's tricks. He was preparing to save his glory, trying to turn a defeat into victory. If he said his chants to the spirits and Jamak lived, then he would gain the praise. If the other died, then he could not be blamed, for he had tried to save this foolish one. It would be a lesson to others not to violate the chief's warnings. He could not lose.

Treek studied Jamak's face. It was a kindly face, not like the evil and cunning one Combuc possessed. He had called Treek his "dearest friend." This was a sign of the bond that had grown between them. Even when the stupidity and ignorance of the People of the River's Bend grieved and sickened him, Jamak gave him a reason to remain. Because Jamak was Jamak. There was so much they could never share. They could not talk together and experience each other's mind, but there was a closeness Treek had thought impossible for non-telepaths. Indeed, Jamak was his friend — but he was more than even that. On Laazed, Treek had never become ready to parent, and, though his canine half had fathered several litters here, those young possessed only a part of him. He'd never passed anything of his full self on to another. Until now. Until this scraggly, unkempt boy-turned-man. Yes, he was certainly a friend. But Jamak had also become his child! And despite all his faults — maybe because of them — he loved this human.

Even as he was gripped by this self-revelation, Treek felt there was something more. He looked again into Combuc's face, then around the campfire at the other hunters. Were they all to become like this? Was Combuc the future of man? With those like him using their wits to dominate and cheat their fellow humans? Would mankind become a race of hucksters and hypocrites? Treek tried to let himself conceive of a future perhaps a million years hence where the intelligent among men used their knowledge to control and destroy their fellow beings. It was not a pretty image. Somehow his mind slipped into the past and picked up the memory of that dead planet bubbling with radioactivity which Jecke told him had once been brimming with life. If those like Combuc came to rule this world, that could be the future here too.

And he knew he could not allow these people to be tricked and conned by the likes of Combuc anymore. In a flash, he sent out thought waves to his friend and "child." Seconds later, Jamak converted those thoughts into words and spat them in Combuc's direction.

"Stop!" he shouted, jumping to his feet. "Don't speak your chants for me. I don't want your help. If this meat is poisoned by evil spirits, as you say, so be it; then I will die. If it isn't poisoned, then I'll live. I will eat and suffer my own fate with no help from you, Combuc. I had no help from you in gathering this meat, and I want no help from you now!"

Good! He had said it. Treek knew he could not have expressed it better himself. Not in the language of these people. Now Jamak had outtricked the trickster. Unless the other came up with still another scheme. Treek was certain that Combuc would not give up easily. Both he and Jamak must be ever on the alert for new trickery now. He was bound to try something else.

Soon Jamak had completed his meal of raw meat. All the other hunters had fasted.

Treek's "master" pulled himself over to his corner of the cave and joined his mate and their little one, but he stopped long enough to pat Treek gently on the head before he lay down with Mawac. Presently, Treek could hear the woman crying.

"You were very foolish, Jamak," he heard her say. "It is as Combuc said. If you were determined to eat that cursed meat, why didn't you let him say his chants and preserve you from this spirits' evil?"

She had spoken very softly so only Treek had overheard the conversation, but Jamak was not soft in his reply. In fact, it was obvious he was deliberately loud so all might hear him.

"What? And let Combuc convince you and all the others with his *lies* that he'd saved me? No, I don't need his saving. If I'm to be saved, let it be by the good spirit which possesses Miskah!"

Oh, if you only knew, Treek wanted to tell him. He was closer to the truth than he could imagine. Yet, he was further from it also. Treek didn't like this talk of "possession." It was one of the things he'd wanted most to defeat in Combuc.

"Hush," Mawac warned her mate. "That dog has gotten you into too much trouble already. Don't let it be the cause of anymore."

## CHAPTER TWENTY-THREE

Treek could hear Jamak's snoring. It did not exactly keep him awake, but he was aware of it. He did not always sleep on the human schedule of daylight and dark. No, sometimes he lay awake half the night listening to the sounds of the jungle animals, both far and near. On other occasions, his mind went seeking backward to a time and place that seemed almost mythical to him now. But he was not dreaming of Laazed tonight. He was remembering what had happened in the last few hours and sorting it out. He knew Mawac had been right in some of the things she'd said and some she hadn't. He was responsible for what had happened. But he hadn't made it happen; he had suggested it only. Jamak was free to decide what he would do. Still, if anything happened to Jamak as a result of what he had encouraged his friend to do...

He dismissed those thoughts of dread and closed his eyes to think back on the time he'd known Jamak. He might be only a savage, but it felt good to hear him say that Treek was his "dearest friend." He was savoring the flavor of that thought. It seemed something he could almost smell and taste as well as feel. It was good. It was the best thing that had happened to him here since he had landed on — and he remembered the phrase he had originally used — "Treek's planet." He saw humor in the thought now. It certainly hadn't turned out to be his world, what with all the calamities that had befallen him. And still...and still it was his. He had roamed its hillsides and forests; he had experienced its summers and winters; he had basked in its sunlight and felt the cold droplets of rain on his back. He had smelled the beauty of flowers, tasted the savory wildlife, heard the delightful songs of its birds, and gloried in all he had seen.

This *was* his world. He had lived here he did not know how long. Was it as long as he'd lived on Laazed? He didn't know — he had lost track of the years so long ago — but he knew it was a long time. Something now urged him to start counting again, and he resolved to do so. But he didn't know why.

Yes, it was *his* world, but at the same time it wasn't. He knew he could never really feel at home here.

Again he felt the old longing. It was still calling him to come home across the stars.

## CHAPTER TWENTY-FOUR

Something was nudging him awake now. Something was tugging at the fringes of his consciousness. Treek put it off and tried to continue sleeping. But he couldn't.

Gradually he opened his eyes. Oh, was that all? He'd seen it hundreds of times before. Why had he awakened just to see Cranic stir the fire?

Wait!

He strained his canine eyes and cursed himself for losing a better set. In the increased glow of the fire, that figure stirring the coals didn't look like the fleet-footed keeper of the flame. No, but it was familiar. Treek strained again trying to get a better look, but still all he could see was the outline. Yet that figure was familiar, hauntingly familiar. He raised his nose into the air, then hesitated, remembering what had happened years ago when Rul still lived. It had taken days to get the smell of smoke out of his nostrils then. But he must know, so he breathed in deeply. The smoke almost choked him, though in that smell — hiding behind it — was another smell. It was hard to pull out and separate because the smoke was so much stronger and pervading, but he knew he must try.

Treek felt himself choking as he took another deep whiff, though he refused to let his throat utter a sound. Yes, now that smell was coming clear, and he liked it even less than he did the smell of smoke.

At the same instant that he identified the scent of the fire-stirrer, he saw the figure turn and start in his direction. Instantly his mind leaped into action. He thrust thoughtwave after thoughtwave outward. He didn't want to move a single muscle just now and provoke something, but he feared the worst. His muscles were rigid, however. He was prepared to lunge at any moment, if necessary, though he preferred not to. Already Jamak was calling him a "good spirit," and he did not feel it wise for his "master" to know he had anything to do with this. Besides, he felt confident that Jamak could handle his own battles now. He must learn to. Treek realized he couldn't go on providing him crutches forever.

Over the years, Treek had learned that the simplest message was often the most effective. So his mind repeated this one over and over, carrying the simplest of all messages:

*"Danger! Danger! Danger! Danger! Danger! Danger! Danger!"* Again and again he repeated it with the full force of his canine brain, and occasionally he would add another word: *"Awaken! Danger! Danger! Danger! Awaken!..."*

He only hoped that Jamak still retained enough anger within his sleeping body to make it possible for him to receive the message.

As the form creeped ever closer to the sleeping Jamak, Treek found his own muscles growing even more tense. He was ready to spring still, but he continued to repeat his message, now faster and with renewed urgency.

The dark figure slowly raised the club he had carried by his side. Instantly Treek was on his feet, but at the exact same moment Jamak quickly rolled over and sprang upward. The dark form's club fell on the vacant ground where his friend had been sleeping.

"No-o-o-o-o-o!"

Treek glanced away from Jamak for a split second, long enough to see Mawac screaming and hugging her child.

Now Jamak was at the other's throat, and the two were rolling around the cave's dirt floor. There were shouts and curses coming from each of the men, and others throughout the cave were coming awake and adding to the din of excitement.

Treek now found it difficult to follow the battle occurring only a few feet away, but he could hear the two men thrashing about. Once he caught a glimmer of that club as it rose in the air and came down with a thud. He heard a grunt at that moment, but the rolling and shouting continued, so he knew the blow had not slain either of the combatants.

Both men were suddenly back on their feet, and Treek thought he could see their faces more clearly. They were pounding and clawing at each other. Blood appeared to cover them both. Yes, he was certain now. He could see the color red. He glanced back and saw dawn's first light streaming in through the cave's mouth, and just at that instant there was another mighty thud.

When he turned his head again, only one man was standing, and he was very still.

Slowly the hairs which had been standing on the back of his neck fell into place. Quietly he walked over to lick the blood from Jamak's hand, and, as he did so, he implanted one final message into his "master's" mind. He knew it should be easy to get through to the other because Jamak must be drenched in emotion. However, he didn't know how his friend would react to this one. It was more complicated than the last, and it required concentration and a reversal of his action, but Treek had hope that Jamak would comply. There was hope for man the species only if he did, for Jamak represented the best potential for this world.

Abruptly Jamak reached down and grasped his opponent's throat and pulled the other man to a standing position. Now dawn's light showed clearly the face that Treek's nostrils had recognized much earlier.

"Combuc!" Jamak shouted. "You are an evil one!"

There was no sound from the other or from anyone else in the cave. Jamak continued to hold the chief up and stare into his ugly, defeated, bloodshot eyes. Quickly, Combuc shifted his gaze downward.

"You are *evil*, Combuc. You have tricked our people since I can remember. You have cheated them. And you have feared them. If you had not been so evil, you would have had no reason to fear any of us."

He flung Combuc back to the floor of the cave where he lay in a patch of blood, but he made no effort to move.

Jamak turned to his fellow hunters and quickly examined their faces. "There he is, the spineless one. What would you do with him?"

Burac was the first to speak, but his cry was quickly picked up by the other hunters.

"Stone him! Stone him!" they shrieked, and their cry was now picked up by the women and children, as well.

"No!" Jamak shouted, drowning out the horde. "We will not kill him, for that's the way he would have acted. But he cannot remain among the People of the River's Bend."

Good! There was *hope* for mankind. Treek watched as the former chief pulled himself to his feet and dragged himself toward the mouth of the cave. He paused only a moment to stare at Kula, but his mate quickly turned her back on him. So he left alone. Not even his children made a move to join their father.

Treek continued to watch as the solitary figure moved

away from the cave, walking toward the rising sun, but steering away from the depths of the jungle — staying in the grassy areas in which he had always led the hunt. Treek heard a jungle cat cry out and saw Combuc jump and stare into the jungle, then continue his march away from the cave.

Straining his dog's eyes, he continued to watch until the old chief disappeared from sight.

## CHAPTER TWENTY-FIVE

And he watched the other hunters hail the new chief. All joined in a feast of the meat which they had brought in the previous day.

It was a day of happiness for Jamak and all the People of the River's Bend, as it should have been for Treek. But it was not.

While he chewed on a deer's leg, Jamak beckoned Treek. "Miskah, come over here and taste the meat of your new chief." He held out a bone with much meat left on it. Treek strolled
forward to accept the gift.

"Take it, It's yours," Jamak urged as Treek reached him. "You've earned it. You'll eat your share. Right, my friends?" He turned to face the other hunters at the cave's mouth. There were grunts of assent all around.

"Miskah, from now on you'll join every hunt. With the good spirit guiding you, and the ability of these men, we will always bring back much food."

But Treek knew it wasn't so.

Jamak laughed uproarously as he continued to stuff himself. He wasn't a pretty sight, still covered in blood from his recent battle. His cuts and bruises were numerous. But these did not douse his spirits.

Jamak again focused his attention on Treek. "Miskah, my friend, I know you're getting old, but you surely must have many hunts left in you."

Gently he licked the hand of this one whom he had befriended so long ago. Now Jamak had befriended him. This "master" would always hold a special place in his heart, he knew.

That night as the hunters and their mates and young ones slept, Treek slipped silently from the cave. It had been his home for many years, and, in it, he had changed many of his attitudes about men, especially one boy-turned-man.

But it was time for him to go.

Jamak no longer needed him as a crutch. He had become the leader of his people. He must make his own decisions from here on, be they wise or foolish, good or ill. Treek thought of the birds he'd seen here, on Laazed, and across the universe. They seemed to be the same everywhere. And when their young ones were grown, the parents pushed them from the nest. Or was this more like a human child learning to walk? Indeed, Jamak was that child, that young bird. He must test his legs/his wings and then solo. The parent could not hover near him forever to catch him if he fell. It was painful, but true. Treek knew that if he remained, he could not resist the temptation to continue offering solutions to Jamak's problems, and that would not help him or his kind grow up. Both Jamak and mankind must learn to run and fly on their own.

Besides, he rationalized, he didn't really want to be a god.

It was a clear night, so finally he paused and gazed up toward the heavens as he had done so often before. He knew he must go on searching for signs of his people's return, and he felt strangely confident. If it took forever, he would not stop. He missed his world and his kind, for he still did not belong here. But he no longer felt angry or lost or betrayed. He did not even feel the need to rush. He would find a way eventually. There was still hope for him.

Something jerked his attention back to the here-and-now. He sniffed the air. His canine nose told him there was a tiger about. He knew he must move on and find shelter soon, but he took time to glance back in the direction of the cave. In the darkness, it was no longer visible, though he could still see it in his mind.

Drops of warm, salty liquid dripped from his eyes and splashed onto the jungle floor.

Into what was almost a mental void he dispatched a message which he was certain his "master" would never receive:

*"Goodbye, Jamak. There IS hope for man, for you have proven it!"*

## EPILOGUE

Susan gently patted "Gray's" head.

In his mind, he smiled as he looked up at her. These humans were not always the most alert pupils, often misconstruing or ignoring many of his thought-projections. There had been some failures, but in 100 centuries, his average of successes far exceeded those who had not reached the mark. And some of his students — his "masters" — had proven their true worth to the world.

Socrates — who, despite his distaste for "science," developed the inquiring mind into a new instrument of competence.

Leonardo — who possessed a very high threshold for telepathy and became one of Treek's most receptive pupils.

Copernicus — who (after Treek's almost 100 centuries of waiting) finally turned man's attention seriously to the stars.

Harriet Beecher Stowe — who pointed the way to value in all mankind.

Thomas Edison — whose light let the world unburden itself.

Martin Luther King, Jr. — who helped others see over the mountaintop of inequality into a valley of brotherhood.

And now there was Susan. Treek realized that she

was speaking, so he withdrew again from his memories.

"Ol' boy, I don't know where you get all that energy. I just wish I knew how old you really are."

She smiled at him, then turned and walked from the porch into the ranchhouse.

The rain had stopped, and the clouds were clearing. The stars were visible, and a bright light came shooting out of the heavens, moving quickly toward the east.

With a bound, Treek left the porch. He was chasing another falling star.

THE END

## ABOUT THE AUTHOR

**Neal Proud Deer** has published millions of words over the course of his career as a staff writer, columnist, critic, and book author. He has also worked as a copy editor, news editor, managing editor, senior editor, and editor/publisher for several newspapers and magazines and has served on three college faculties.

More than 60 of his celebrity profiles have appeared on magazine covers, with interviews of such notables as President Jimmy Carter, poet Maya Angelou, actor Leonard Nimoy, baseball great Ozzie Smith, singers Peter, Paul & Mary, billionaire Steve Fossett, feminist and author Betty Friedan, television late-night host Jay Leno, comedian and social activist Bill Cosby, and Secretary of State Madeleine Albright.

His recent non-fiction book *Lights…Camera…Arch!* includes a foreword by award-winning film and television star John Goodman, and his book *Selling's Magic Words* was a major national seller in the 1980's and was utilized from coast to coast as a text by colleges and universities such as Purdue, California State, and the City University of New York.

His short fiction has appeared in print in various publications since the late 1960's. And his two sons are filmed screenwriters and staged playwrights living in Los Angeles.

Printed in the United States
133721LV00005B/6/P

9 781604 814101